"This book is destined to be another spiritual classic by the author of *The Dark Night of Recovery*. In *The Seven Deadly Needs*, the irreverent Tyler continues the dialogue with humor and wisdom, this time illustrating the fact that emotional and spiritual transformation consists of removing obstacles or 'needs' that prevent us from living as the spiritual beings we are. It is an enlightening and entertaining 'manual' with more steps toward health and wholeness."

—Judith G. Dowling, Psy.D., clinical pyschologist

"A wonderful, thought-provoking read, filled with guidance from one who understands the path toward absolute surrender. Simple and clear, it provides guidance and a way to see beyond our shortcomings—and to learn principles that foster love of self and of others."

—Linda C. Wilson, M.S.W., C.A.C.I.I.

"*The Seven Deadly Needs* is a delightful book about how to get free, how to deal with fear, and how to surrender to the Divine Intelligence that connects us all. It takes a closer look at how our 'deadly needs' are obstacles that keep us from enjoying life. I plan to recommend this book to all my clients."

—Donna Strickland, M.D., R.N., C.S.,
national speaker, organizational development consultant
(www.DonnaStrickland.com)

D1118175

THE SEVEN DEADLY
NEEDS

Edward Bear

White River Press
Amherst, Massachusetts

THE SEVEN DEADLY NEEDS

Edward Bear

published January 2008 by White River Press
by arrangement with the author

publication history
Health Communications, Inc.
copyright © 2000

cover art by JC Davis

cover design by Sonja Hakala

White River Press
PO Box 3561
Amherst, MA 01004
www.whiteriverpress.com

ISBN: 978-0-9792451-7-6

Library of Congress Cataloging-in-Publication Data
Bear, Edward, 1938-2005.
  The seven deadly needs / Edward Bear.
    p. cm.
  ISBN 978-0-9792451-7-6 (pbk. : alk. paper)
  1. Recovery movement--Fiction. 2. Imaginary conversations.
3. Psychological fiction. I. Title.
  PS3569.L267S48 2008
  813'.54--dc22
                                        2007046589

To the Elder Bears, gone long ago to the Great Forest.

Jo, who tends the hearth with love and joy.

*The children—Tom (wherever you are),
Tree, Cat, Monica, Laura, Steve.*

*Judith, healer and angel,
cleverly disguised as a person.*

*The Community, whose warmth
is shelter from the cold.*

*All those from York Street to
Cherry Creek who carry the Message
without thought of reward.*

Someday, after we have mastered the winds, the waves, the tides and gravity, we shall harness for God the energies of love. Then, for the second time in the history of the world, mankind will have discovered fire.

—Pierre Teilhard de Chardin

A man stood before God, his heart breaking from the pain and injustice in the world.
"Dear God," he cried, "Look at all the suffering, the anguish, the distress in your world. Why don't you send help?"
And God said: "I did send help. I sent you."

—David Wolpe
Teaching Your Children About God

"Come to the cliff," he said.
They said, "We are afraid."
"Come to the cliff," he said.
They came. He pushed them. And they flew.

—Old French Proverb

This is what you shall do: Love the earth and the sun and the animals, despise riches, give alms to everyone that asks, stand up for the stupid and the crazy, devote your income and labor to others, hate tyrants, argue not concerning God. . . .

—Walt Whitman

The eye goes blind when it only wants to see why.

—Rumi

CONTENTS

PROLOGUE

*You teach best what you most
need to learn.*

—Richard Bach, *Illusions*

Nobody knows how long he's lived here, maybe not even
Tyler himself. But most everybody knows him. At least
knows who he is. Claims he's been here sixty-some years, but
you can't get anybody to swear to it. I mean besides him. Never
met anyone who actually remembers him from when they
were young. Going to school with him. Anything like that.
It's possible that Tyler never *was* young. I think about
that sometimes. Just seems like he's always been here, like
the town itself.

Despite the fact that he can be difficult at times, he is gen-
erally held in high regard by most people. There are those
who say (though certainly not a majority) that he has about

him a certain aura of wisdom, an assessment he would most assuredly reject. But he looks the part—tall, gray, a little bent with age, his face a leathery map of what could pass for wisdom. Trouble is, he is more likely to act like a juvenile delinquent than someone with a little wisdom—getting into snowball fights with the neighborhood kids, going to *The Rocky Horror Picture Show* at midnight at least once a month. (It's been rumored that some parents don't want their kids hanging around him, but I never heard any of the kids complain. They all seem to love him.)

A few of the townspeople are convinced that he's a little shaky in the mental department, a few bricks short of a full load so to speak, or at best an old man who gives new meaning to the word eccentric. (They would be even more appalled if they knew the Real Story.) The town's very old-fashioned about things like that. Very conservative. They feel that a person well past the half-century mark should conduct himself with a certain amount of dignity. And dignified, he is not. What Tyler always says is, *Nobody I know of is getting out of this thing alive, so why not enjoy it? Besides, you'd be surprised at what's waiting on the other side.* . . . Whatever that last part means.

I know him from the meetings we go to. I'm not allowed to say which ones, but they are Twelve-Step type meetings that are supposed to be anonymous. You know—recovery stuff. Hence the fact that I refer to him as Tyler (not his real name) and myself as Edward Bear (not my real name, either). It says in one of those books we read that, *Anonymity is the spiritual foundation of all our traditions.* . . . Has a real nice ring to it, though the meaning is a little hazy. Tyler says it means you're just supposed to suit up and show up and not make a big deal about it. The names and identities of the guilty or innocent are unimportant. The fact that you're clean and sober, not eating a whole chocolate cake for breakfast, not gambling away the rent money, or having a dozen orgasms a day to relieve the tension ought to be reward enough. Means you're doing a few things right. Enough things.

Progress, not perfection, is what he says, grinning like everybody should know what that means. *It's hard by the yard, but a cinch by the inch.* Another one of his corny favorites.

But he's a guy who just seems to be there when you need him. I remember during my divorce when I didn't think I was going to make it, Tyler would just show up someplace where I was. Out of the blue, there he was. Or he'd call. *How are you and that divorce lawyer doing?*

You know during that time I even thought about killing myself. Got to be way too much for me. That's right, old Mr. Stability himself, Steady Eddy Bear, thought about ending it all. Here I was, college educated (so what if I didn't get through all four years?), with a regular job as checker at the local Safeway (where I got my real education), unpublished writer-in-residence, actually a pretty stable guy, and I was thinking about pulling down the final curtain a little early. Tyler said I'd probably end up killing the wrong guy. I didn't get what he meant until a year later.

Tyler was in the habit of chuckling about it. There is no misfortune so tragic that Tyler can't find some humor in it. So he suggested (we don't *tell* one another to do things in recovery, we *suggest*—works better that way) that I might want to get back to basics and do some of those Twelve Steps again. I hated it. Every week another step, and old Tyler just chuckling away like it's the funniest thing that ever happened. Here I am dying, my wife's throwing me out of the house and Tyler's going *ha ha ha*. . . .

But before we were through I began to feel better. Almost in spite of myself. Tyler always talks about life being a series of surrenders. It's simple, he says. You get beat up enough, you surrender or you die. When I ask what I need to surrender, or who I need to surrender to, he just shrugs and says he doesn't have a clue. *But you know,* he says, that long, crooked finger pointed at my chest. Personally, I think he knows and just won't tell me.

So the latest thing is I get a letter in the mail. I mean I see him at least twice a week, and he finds it necessary to send me a letter. Can't just talk to me. Tyler has to send a letter. This is what it says:

Dear Anonymous:

I'll be at your house this Thursday at seven. And for the next seven Thursdays. Get some tapes for your portable recorder. We will be discussing one of the Seven Deadly Needs on each of those Thursdays. You will have questions about them. I know you will. Because you're smart. The Seven Deadly Needs are as follows:

The need to KNOW
The need to BE RIGHT
The need to GET EVEN
The need to LOOK GOOD
The need to JUDGE

The need to KEEP SCORE
The need to CONTROL

. . . not necessarily in the order of importance.
(Later he tells me a long, involved story about how
the Seven Deadly Needs came to him in a dream. Like a
vision. At best I am suspicious; at worst I think it is an outright fabrication.)

He doesn't even sign it, but I know it's from him. Who else
could it be? Nobody is who else. Only Tyler would send a letter like that, assuming that I would rearrange my life in
whatever way was necessary to set aside the next seven
Thursdays. Just for him. So he could come and talk about
the Seven Deadly Needs or whatever. But of course I do. I
know it's important. He talks a lot now about the fact that
his time here is short (he tells me I'm his replacement, so he
may have to accelerate my training). He says he's preparing
to return to the Source, to go home to the Big Pumpkin
Patch in the Sky and be reunited with what he refers to as
the Great Pumpkin. Talk about crazy ideas. *Where it's
Halloween all the time and everyone dresses up to play
"Treat or Treat."* Drives the religious people crazy. He is
irreverent at best, sacrilegious at worst. He has been known
to use the F-word in close conjunction with the G-word.
Like right next to it in a sentence. Out loud. Now that seriously drives some people crazy. But I know him well enough
to know that he does it to make people think about what
they actually believe. At least I think that's why he does it.
Maybe he just likes to shock people. Hard to tell with Tyler.

But make no mistake, I love the guy, though I continue to
give him a hard time about almost everything. I even

question the things he says that I know are true. I recognize it as Truth Itself, but I still have a question or two. Just to keep him on his toes. Guy like him could get complacent.

So what follows are the recorded sessions of the Seven Deadly Needs, taped during the Thursday Evening Coffee Hour, with occasional editorial comments by your friendly reporter. Uncut and uncensored, if not unplugged. And Tyler's still here, but I don't think for long.

One

The Need to Know

Imagination is more important than knowledge.

—Albert Einstein

Sometimes he comes over and just sits for a while. Doesn't say a word. We sit in the basement in my study (where I'm supposed to be writing but am more often reading some mind-numbing adventure story or deeply involved in exploring something totally irrelevant on the Internet. Anything but actually writing). We sit and breathe. Tyler is very big on breathing. His answer to the really deep, philosophical issues of our time is often, *Just keep breathing*. He actually says things like that. So I am usually not surprised at what happens when he shows up. And I have done my homework; I have questions about these Seven Deadly Needs he wants to talk about. To discuss.

"So what is it about this need to know?" said Tyler.

(I shrug—the question seems rhetorical.)

"I mean why do I have to know everything?" he said. "Absolutely everything. You think maybe it's some kind of a sickness, Mr. Bear? What is it about knowing things that makes me feel better? You know that's the main reason I'm not hooked up to the Internet. Know what would happen if I was?"

"Probably the same thing that happens to me," I said. "I go off on a tangent and waste hours trying to uncover some obscure historical fact that has absolutely no relevance. Like who Galileo's mother was."

"Mrs. Galileo."

"Her name."

"Mama Galileo."

"Jesus, Tyler."

"So why is it we have to know everything?"

I hedged a little. I didn't want to make the whole thing too easy for him.

"I'm not so sure I have to know everything," I said. "Not everything."

"You're an exception?"

"I mean *some* things, yeah, but . . ."

"Mrs. Galileo?"

"Well . . . That's just the Internet."

"But most things?" He wouldn't let it go. "Don't you have this . . . this thing inside you that tells you that you have to know why things are the way they are? Or why things happen the way they do? Or when? Don't you have that nagging little voice that says, *A really smart person would know why that happened?* Or, *If I knew that I'd be better off. Or safer at least.* Doesn't that go on inside you? In some secret place?"

"Well . . ."

"You know, that was what caused all that trouble in the Garden of Eden."

"What was?"

"The need to know," said Tyler. "You remember the snake saying to Eve, *You see that tree in the middle of the Garden with all the fruit on it? The one God doesn't want you to eat from? Well, Eve, that's the Tree of Knowledge, and if you eat the fruit of that tree your eyes will be opened, and you'll be just like God. I mean, God's no dummy—just look at all this stuff. You'll become absolutely brilliant. You want to be brilliant, don't you? Everybody wants to be brilliant. Not to mention pretty. Don't you want to know things? Impress Adam?*"

"I didn't know you were a big Bible guy," I said. "Rumor has it that you're more of an agnostic."

"Don't believe all the rumors," he said. "Basically, I'm neutral about the whole thing, but I remember a few things from Sunday school. So she eats the fruit and gives some to Adam. Then her eyes are opened, and she notices that they're both naked. Here's the part they never tell you. Adam already knew they were naked, but didn't let on. And of course they get caught because there's only two of them and God doesn't have much else to do but spy on them. So Adam blames Eve, and Eve blames the serpent, and they have to leave the Garden of Eden because . . . because . . . ?"

"Because they had to know everything."

"Right. The need to know. It's a disease. Even the snake has to leave. Even the snake for chrissakes. That's what the need to know does for you."

"Doesn't sound good."

"It's terrible. We're talking paradise here, and they have to leave because Eve has to know everything."

"It's her fault?" I said. "We don't blame women for everything anymore, Tyler. It's the new thing."

"I'm not blaming her," said Tyler. "I'm just repeating the story. She ate the fruit and gave some to Adam. *Here, Adam, this is really good.* That's what the story says. I didn't write it. . . . So what's the question you're dying to ask?"

"What makes you think I have a question?"

"I know you have a question. You actually *are* brilliant. Ever since you stopped taking that Prozac, you've been much better."

"I never took Prozac, Tyler. You know that. I just talked about the *possibility*. Discussed it. Unfortunately, I discussed it with you."

"You mean *fortunately* you discussed it with me," said Tyler. "I was able to spot the flaw in your thinking and redirect your recovery into healthier channels."

"Thank you, Mr. Tyler."

"Tranquilizers are out."

"They're not tranquilizers," I said. "They're antidepressants. There's a difference."

"Semantics," he said.

Tyler can be very stubborn and narrow-minded about some things. This is one. He thinks that because he didn't need them, nobody should need them. He pictures himself as one of the craziest people to ever land in recovery, and since he didn't need them, nobody else should either. Of course they didn't have antidepressants when he got started, something he conveniently overlooks. When pressed on the issue, he will grudgingly admit that some people, *a few* people in his opinion, might actually need them. The rest, he believes, are seeking an easier, softer way. *Better living through chemistry*, he grumbles.

"No, it's not semantics," I said, holding my ground.

"What happened to a spiritual solution?"

"You can still have it."

"Not likely," he said. "How about Gandhi on Prozac? Can you imagine? India would still be part of the British Empire."

"Apples and oranges," I said.

"Or Winston Churchill?"

"Stop already. I give up. It's a circular argument."

"How so?" he said.

"We just keep going 'round and 'round."

"That's because you have failed to grasp the truth of what I'm saying. You remember King's speech in Washington?"

(Though he has trouble remembering what night the Thursday Night meeting is, for some odd reason he can quote large portions of speeches by the famous and infamous. Same with books.)

"No, but you're going to tell me about it, right?"

"Only the last part. *Free at last! Free at last! Thank God Almighty, we are free at last! . . . Now if you'll excuse me, I have to take my Prozac.*"

"Tyler, Tyler," I said. "That's very transparent."

"Transparent. Sometimes the truth is transparent, and you miss it. You look right through it to the lie on the other side."

"What if I told you I was suicidal? That I wanted to kill myself?"

"As your part-time mentor, I'd advise against it," he said. "Very poor solution to whatever the problem is."

"What if the only thing that would help me was an antidepressant?"

"You've tried everything and nothing helped? And you still want to kill yourself?"

"I've tried everything."

"I find it hard to believe you've tried every . . ."

"Don't be evasive, Tyler. For the sake of the argument, I've tried everything."

Tyler seemed to be staring at something just above my head.

"Then you take the antidepressant."

"Thank you," I said.

"Thank you for what?" said Tyler. "It's a no-brainer. You always choose life."

"So what's the beef with Prozac?"

"The beef is that people think it's okay to take it after they've had a bad day at the office, or when the old bowling average sinks below a hundred, or when their Fantasy Football team had a tough week."

"And you don't think that's okay."

"Right. I don't think that's okay."

"Is that like being in the judgment business?" I said. It makes him crazy when I accuse him of judging people. So I do it every chance I get. I like to think it helps keep him spiritually fit. He probably wouldn't agree.

"Sometimes when I look at you," said Tyler, "I feel like

Dr. Frankenstein. I've created this monster that's going to haunt me for the rest of my life."

"Thank you."

"I'm not sure that was meant to be a compliment."

"I accept anyway," I said.

"And, though it pains me to admit it," he said, "you're probably right about the judgment business. What I need to do is honor your journey, not judge it." He looked up at the ceiling and sighed. "Another serious character defect surfaces. Will it never end?"

He sighed again, "Besides, I have no idea what your lesson plan is. As a matter of fact, I have very little idea what my own lesson plan is. However, and this is very important, if it seems to me that you're walking toward a Burmese tiger trap without being aware of it, I would feel compelled to point that out. With or without checking your Lesson Plan."

"I love being right."

"I know," he said dryly. "If you'll check the list of needs, you'll find out that the need to be right has a very prominent place. If I'm not mistaken, it's the very next one."

"Ready for the question?" I said.

"Ready." He sounded weary.

"The question is, What's the most important thing I *don't* need to know?" I said.

"That you *don't* need to know?"

Tyler closed his eyes for a moment.

"I bet you were the kind of child who wanted to know why the sky was blue? You probably asked your parents that. *Why is the sky blue, Mommy?* Or, *Why don't your eyes fall out, Daddy?* The kind of child who was always sticking his finger in people's noses because you were curious about noses. I mean if you're small and you're looking up into those big faces with noses that are like cavities, they do become a curiosity. Were you that way?"

"I don't remember."

"I bet you were," he said. "I was. With me it was feet. When I was little, I'd sit on the kneeler in church and stare at all the shoes under the pew in front of me. Fascinated by all the different kinds of shoes. I didn't get into trouble 'til I started untying the laces. I didn't know they belonged to people; as far as I could tell they were just shoes and little short legs.

"Then later in catechism, when they started talking about eternity, I was the one kid who had to know how long it was. How long eternity was. Nobody else seemed to care, but it kept going 'round and 'round in my head. Couldn't stop thinking about it. *Forever,* they said. *That's how long.* Well, forever wasn't a very satisfying answer. They absolutely insisted that it would never end, heaven or hell. And it always seemed to me that it absolutely *had* to end. Whatever it was. Then I started writing down all the numbers I knew because they said if I added up all the numbers in the world it would not even be one day in eternity. Not even the beginning of one day. I had pages and pages full of numbers. Finally I just started adding zeroes. Then I had pages and pages of zeroes."

"Long time," I said.

"Yes . . . But not eternity. Eternity not only has no ending, they further confused the issue by telling me it didn't have a beginning either."

"It just . . . always was?"

"Apparently."

"Hard to believe," I said.

He thought about that for a moment.

"You could say that."

"I just did."

"Didn't you tell me that you didn't have much religious training in your younger years?"

"Occasional Sunday school was about it," I said. "I'm the only person I ever heard of who got suspended from Sunday school for behavior problems. And I did twice."

"Nice to get an early start on those behavior problems," he said. "But look on the bright side: There's less to unlearn. At a very early age, young Catholics are given a full load of unsolvable mysteries to ponder for the rest of their lives. Very grim. We have a virgin birth, which only started to bother me after I found out what virgin meant and what birth meant. Then there was eternity, hell, the Ascension, Original Sin, the Immaculate Conception, some others that I can't recall at the moment. Cosmic dilemmas just crying out to be resolved. There's something about cosmic dilemmas that absolutely terrifies the preadolescent mind. I can remember one year it rained a lot, and I was worried that we were all going to drown because God was going to send another flood. You remember Noah?"

"Who could forget Noah?"

"I was actually relieved when my sister told me that next time the world was going to end by fire. God had already done the water thing, so the next time it would be fire. Didn't want people to get bored with the same old catastrophes. I don't know why, but I felt better just knowing that. Maybe it's because I'm claustrophobic. I get panicky just thinking about drowning."

"But at least I believe in God," I said. "Unlike some people I know."

"The rumor that I don't believe in God has been grossly exaggerated, perhaps started by some malcontent who noticed that I don't say the Lord's Prayer at the end of meetings. Fact is, I do believe in God. I just don't call the God I believe in God, that's all. At least not usually."

"I'll stop before we get lost. So the most important thing I *don't* need to know is?"

"The most important thing you *don't* need to know is why things happen the way they do. You don't need to know that. Nobody needs to know that. Very important point. Here's what somebody said about the subject: *Make no judgments . . . Give up the need to know why things happen as they do.* 'Why' is not such a good word. Why and when. Once you get into why and when, it's all over. The Big Brain, the sick ego-driven brain that has to know absolutely everything, takes over and goes 'round and 'round until it destroys itself. Overheats and burns out. Essentially, it thinks itself to death. It's the intellectual equivalent of a dog chasing its tail. Horrible. And once it starts, you can't stop it."

"Man . . ."

"Not a pretty picture," said Tyler.

"I guess not," I said. "Death by thinking. . . . Now for the last question. What's the most important thing I *do* need to know?"

"Hmmm . . . The most important thing you *do* need to know is that knowing things is vastly overrated. Information for the sake of information. Your head can be so full of facts that you forget you have a heart. We are literally drowning in facts. Being smothered. I now have enough information to last three lifetimes. At least. Facts. God, save me from more facts. Hearts are what count. We forget that information is available from other sources."

"That's it? That's all I need to know?"

"Well, not quite. It's also important to know that the universe inclines toward you. It wishes you well. It is of good intent."

"Of good intent," I said. "The universe is . . . is God?"

"Could be," said Tyler.

"So when you say universe, you mean something that *could be* God?"

"God," said Tyler, grimacing slightly. "Not a great word for me. Conjures up images of judgment, damnation, fire and brimstone."

"So what do you call it, this . . . universe you're talking about?"

"I change names for it every few years. In the beginning it was cosmic consciousness. Universal mind during my intellectual period. The Great Spirit, which I still use sometimes. The Force. I like that—the Force. *May the Force be with you.* Remember that?"

"And your current designation?" I said.

"I've been using the Great Pumpkin the last couple of years."

"A comic strip character," I said. "You pray to a comic strip character?"

"What makes you think that the Great Pumpkin is just a comic strip character?" said Tyler.

"Because it's in a *cartoon*, Tyler. A comic strip *cartoon*. In the papers. Peanuts. Might as well be Dilbert. Why don't you pray to Dilbert?"

"Get serious," he said. "Dilbert doesn't fit the bill. Just look at him. Besides, what's wrong with using a cartoon character for a higher power? Especially one like the Great Pumpkin. Keep in mind that he has a lot of power, and nobody has ever seen him. Sound familiar?"

"It just seems . . . goofy," I said. "Juvenile. We're talking God here, Tyler, not Mickey Mouse."

"People take religion far too seriously," said Tyler, shaking his head. "I suspect that the Great Pumpkin has a much better sense of humor than we give him credit for. Or her . . . And just what does all this have to do with the Need to Know?"

"Everything," I said. "What's more important than knowing if there really is a God?"

"Lots of things."

"Like what?"

"Like how is your life today? Are you gambling away the rent money again? Are you clean and sober today? Are you yelling at your spouse again? Did you have a *whole* chocolate cake for breakfast? Did you . . . ?"

"That's more important than knowing whether there's a God?"

"Of course. If you're loaded on drugs or food or sex or wallowing in self-pity or yelling at people all the time, what difference does it make if there's a God or not? Your Higher Power is something else anyway. Besides, at some core level, everybody knows. The cells in your body, the molecules themselves, know they're connected to a . . ."

"But . . ."

"Don't make it any more complicated than it is," said Tyler. "It's very simple. It goes like this: There is a Power. Doesn't make any difference what you call It. That Power is not you, though you are a part of it. You have access to it. It may work through you and through others. Now if you believe that there's a God, or a Higher Power, one is more likely to show up in your life. I mean more likely than if you *don't* believe. But it's there whether you believe it or not. It's like believing in miracles. If you believe in miracles, you have a much better chance of experiencing one."

"You're saying that I'm creating God by believing in him? Creating miracles?"

"No, I'm saying that you have a better chance of *experiencing* them if you believe. Does that offend your intellectual sensibilities?"

Sometimes I wonder where he comes up with this stuff.

"Frankly, yes," I said.

"Doesn't surprise me," he said. "Being bright has its drawbacks, too. You not only seem to have this need to know about everything, but the need to know in a certain way, a way that's intellectually satisfying. *Your way,* in other words. Sinatra had a song about it. Only he called it 'My Way.' Same thing. Referred to in some circles as intellectual arrogance."

"No, I . . ."

"Yes, yes," he interrupted. "You want to build a fence around this power so you can study it, dissect it, find out what makes It tick so you can be . . . what?"

"What do you mean, be what?"

"Why would you want to study this Power, find out what makes it tick, how it works?"

"I never said I wanted to do that. *You're* the one who . . ."

"Let me help," he said. "The reason you want to do that is because if you can dissect it, study it, you will eventually be able to explain it, and ultimately be *safe* because you can control it. Hence, control is the seventh and deadliest need. The need to control is the bedrock of all the deadly needs. But, more about that later."

"Doesn't all this strike you as somewhat simplistic?" I said.

"No," he said. "Just because it's simple doesn't mean it's simplistic. Basic is a better word. The premise is that life works from the inside out, not the other way around. You ever hear that phrase: *It's an inside job?* That's what it means. Experience follows expectation. If you expect miracles, they'll show up. They are all around us, waiting to be acknowledged."

"Funny I didn't notice any."

"They are in the silence between the words, between the thoughts. You may be too busy to notice."

"Ah . . . the silence."

"Pandering to the need to know by devouring more and more information doesn't mean anything other than that you may end up being a better Trivial Pursuit player. Also, it may make you less of a person."

"You think I wasted my time going to college?"

"I didn't say *learning* was useless," he said. "I said that gathering facts because you have this need to know the why and when of everything is perhaps not the healthiest of occupations."

There are times when I'm totally mystified by what he appears to think of as logic.

I drank my coffee while Tyler lit another cigarette. He is one of the few people I know who still smokes. Tyler and my ex-wife, Ann.

"Do you remember if Frankenstein's monster had a heart?" I said.

"I believe so," he said. "Some used model out of a graveyard."

"But he did have a heart. The monster did."

"Yes," he said.

"Now the big question. Did the good Dr. Frankenstein himself have a heart?"

The grin took a little while to form.

"What are you saying? I'm belaboring the point? I'm heartless?"

"I have a terrible headache, and there's a trickle of blood coming out of my ear. What do you think?"

"I was only trying to explain that the need to know can be treacherous. Pursued with a certain kind of intensity that many of us seem to possess, it can be deadly."

"I think you said that. Addressed that. Very well, actually."

"You're surrendering?"

"This white flag I'm waving indicates unconditional surrender."

"Good," he said. "The proper response. Life is a series of surrenders. Remember?"

"How could I forget?"

"Got any more coffee? Half a cup would do."

"For you, anything," I said.

"You are the soul of generosity."

"Thank you. You know, Tyler, you are slowly but surely destroying my intellectual life."

"Good. Means we're right on track. When we get through with that, we'll begin on your emotional life and then get to your spiritual life."

"Then I won't have anything left."

"Right." He seemed so cheerful about it. "You'll be a pile of rubble. Loose stones and other debris scattered over the landscape."

"Then what?" I said.

"We rebuild," he said. "Out of the ashes comes the City of God."

"You just said *God*," I reminded him.

"I know. I'm trying to get used to it."

"You think that's possible?" I said. "I mean out of the ashes like that? The City of God?"

"I can see it already," he said. "The cathedral spires are just breaking through the top level of ashes."

"The City of God."

"Come with me," he said, "the best is yet to be."

"Robert Browning?" I said.

"That's the trouble with you literary types," he said. "Can't slide in a quote that I can claim as my own."

He took only a few sips of coffee before he got up to leave.

"Next week, the need to be right," he said. "Ring any bells?"

"Some," I said.

"Good," he said. "In the meantime keep in mind what the Tao says: *The more you know, the less you understand.*"

I nodded as if I understood.

"May the Force be with you," he said. "And the Great Pumpkin."

"Thank you. . . . I love you." It's taken me years to be able to say that. It always seemed so . . . awkward, so alien. The words themselves—I love you. I never heard my father say them. To anybody. Not even my mother. *Men*, I think, shaking my head. *Why is it all so difficult?*

"I love you, too," he said. "Day at a time, my friend. Each day a little miracle."

"The best is yet to be," I said.

He nodded as he walked out the door.

"It's true."

Two

The Need to Be Right

I don't know about you, but God's will for me is trial and error.

—Anonymous

So what is it this week?" I said. "What need?"

"You have the list?" he said.

"Not with me. But since you wrote it, I thought you'd be able to come up with it right off the top."

"Sometimes I have trouble remembering things," said Tyler.

"I know."

"You do, too?"

"No. I just know you do."

"Sometimes," he said. "Some things I remember very well."

"Okay. We'll go with sometimes."

"Not always."

"I got it, Tyler. I got it. . . . Sometimes. Jesus . . ."

"It's coming to me," he said.

"What is?"

He closed his eyes.

"The second deadly need . . ."

"You're having a vision?" I said.

He opened one eye for a moment, then closed it.

"It's the need to be right," he said.

"I knew that," I said.

"You knew that? Knew what it was and you didn't tell me?"

"I didn't tell you because I was helping you exercise your memory. Keep it active. You know, what you don't use, you lose. Nature's way."

"Do me a favor?" he said.

"Anything."

"Don't help. Unless I ask . . . "

"Okay. You want some coffee?"

"I love coffee," he said.

"You know coffee's not supposed to be great for memory problems."

"I have occasional memory lapses. Occasional. Very normal. And actually, as you know, my memory is very good for certain things."

"Trivia," I suggested.

"Wise sayings from the spiritually enlightened are normally not considered trivia."

"Coffee destroys brain cells. By the millions. Proven fact." I knew this line of reasoning was guaranteed to get him going.

"God spare me from facts."

"It's the caffeine," I said.

"What's the caffeine?"

"The part of the coffee that's not healthy. That destroys the brain cells."

"You have a bad day at the office?" he said.

"You could tell?"

"It's fairly obvious," he said dryly. "Do you realize that every day you live shortens your life by one day?"

"That a trick question?"

"No. Proven fact. As the man said, 'You could look it up.'"

"Of course I realize that. A no-brainer, as you might say. But what if every day you drank real coffee shortened your life by *two* days?"

"An acceptable risk. We are not talking about living forever on the Earth plane, Edward. Most everyone I know is leaving someday. Even you. We are talking about enjoying life."

"Coffee's a drug."

"So is aspirin," he said. "And why this sudden, in-depth inquiry into my coffee habit?"

"No inquiry," I said. "Just a discussion of facts. Known, proven facts."

"Such as?"

"Coffee is a drug. Caffeine, actually. If you stop drinking coffee suddenly you will have withdrawal symptoms. Headaches, the whole thing. Since decaf has less caffeine than regular coffee, it is therefore better for you. Although not good by a long shot."

"So you no longer drink coffee?" he said.

"An occasional decaf."

"And of course you don't smoke anymore."

"Of course."

"I see you have taken the moral high ground on this issue. Assumed the moral high ground, as it were, and are now defending it with every ounce of moral fiber available."

The way he said it sounded like an accusation.

"You should get a soapbox," he said. "Set it up in the park. Teach people the difference between right and wrong. Help them."

"Just facts, Tyler."

"Facts meaning truth? Being right?"

"Hey, dead brain cells are dead brain cells. They can measure those."

"Lucky we've got trillions," he said. "You'll never miss a few million."

"You're missing the point," I said.

"You want me to say you're right?"

"It's only a formality. The truth is, I *am* right."

"I wonder what it is about the need to be right that's so . . . comforting?"

"It's not the need to be right," I said. "It's actually *being* right. There's a difference."

"How does being right make you feel?" he said.

"I don't know if it makes me feel anything. I mean you're either right or you're not. Either right or wrong."

"No gray areas?"

"Well . . ."

"When I was young," said Tyler, "I was always trying to prove that my father was wrong. Primarily because he was always right. Or claimed that he was. Got to be a very important part of my life. So I'd try to trap him, catch him in a lie, maybe mispronouncing a word, or telling me about the Olympics in 1932 which he claimed to have attended, when I knew he hadn't. I knew that. I was right. But he would never admit it."

"Not an unfamiliar story."

"I would get the dictionary out and *show* him that he was mispronouncing a word. Show him right in the dictionary. Black and white. The *tilde* the *umlaut*, everything. Sound it out. There, you see? But he'd say the dictionary was wrong. Old edition, he'd say. I'd get a newer edition. I actually did that—bought a newer edition. He'd say that the word was typically pronounced the way he pronounced it because of the regional flavor (always the East Coast guy) and that long usage had made his pronunciation correct. Regardless of what the dictionary said."

"He never gave in?"

"Never," said Tyler. "Held on right to the end."

"What was the end like?"

Tyler took a deep breath.

"Cirrhosis is what it said on the death certificate. Cirrhosis of the liver brought on by chronic alcoholism. I found him in the back room of their little duplex up in Ventura. My mother was hysterical. There he was, belly up, bloated, no clothes on. A fat, dead drunk. I remember the smell, the stench of bourbon and . . . whatever else there was. A small army of ants was crawling across his upper lip, just under the nose. Close-order drill maybe, carrying crumbs from all those crackers he always ate in bed. Ants are very disciplined, you know. Very industrious. I stared at the ants for a long time."

"Jesus . . ."

"King Charles . . . only fifty-three years old when he died.
Long live the king. You know, I wanted to smash him in the
face I was so angry. Dead King Charles had escaped, and he
would never be wrong. Never. That's one of the reasons I had
such a powerful need to be right."

"So you'd be okay?"

"Maybe," he said. "Maybe being right meant that I was
grown up, a man at last. That I somehow belonged. That I
had been adopted into this mystical fellowship of men. That
I had finally achieved something, done something right for a
change. Isn't that what we all want when we're little? Isn't
that what we're all urged to do? Grow up and be men. Here's
another question that never got answered: What's a man?"

"Slow down," I said. "I'm still working on the need to be
right. You ever make your peace with all that? Your dad and
all?"

"Eventually," said Tyler. "Every year around the time he
died, I'd write him a letter detailing all the things I'd always
wanted to say to him. All the things I wanted him to say to me."

"Did it work?"

"After twenty-eight years, twenty-eight letters, on the
anniversary of the twenty-ninth, I wrote him a letter asking
his forgiveness for all the ways I had failed him as a son."

"What happened?" I said.

"It all went away. The resentments, the anger, everything.
Just gone."

"You think just because you wrote that last letter?"

"I don't know," he said. "I know that at some level I
stopped blaming him. Stopped feeling that I had to be right.
That helped. Found out it didn't make any difference who

was right. Just worked my side of the street for a change. Turns out that being right is not terribly important."

"God," I said. "Twenty-nine letters. Twenty-nine *years.*"

"How about you? You have all that right-wrong stuff when you were a kid?"

"You know I don't remember much of what it was like when I was a kid."

"Surprise, surprise."

"Just little flashes like snapshots. There's no continuity. I'm three years old. I'm five years old. I'm in school. One of the few things I remember was that on the first day of school, I set my new lunchpail behind a car and somebody backed over it. All that was left was this flat little round thing with peanut butter oozing out the sides. I loved peanut-butter sandwiches. . . ."

"Aha," said Tyler. "And you were soon informed that you had done something wrong?"

"I think the exact words were—*It's a pretty stupid kid who would leave his lunchpail behind a car.*"

"Of course."

"My father had this quaint way of saying it—*You're a wrong-o, kid.* You ever heard of that? Somebody being called that? A wrong-o? I never heard anybody but my dad say that."

"Only in bad detective novels," he said. "The need to be right is a consequence of always being wrong. Or being led to believe that you were always wrong."

"I even remember what that lunchpail looked like *before* it got run over. I only had it one day, and I can still remember it. Almost forty years ago."

"I bet you can."

"It was a great lunchpail. Painted to look like a train. Kind of oval. Caboose on one end, engine on the other. Little metal handle. And the engine was a face. Not one of those stupid train faces but a real smiling engine face. You know the kind. A face like *The Little Engine That Could.* Happy."

"I do," said Tyler.

"It was my first day in first grade. I'd been to kindergarten, so it wasn't a big deal. Only when I got on the playground, I set my lunchpail down behind a car and went to play dodgeball. What did I know? Six years old. By the way, I was a terrific dodgeball player. They could never get me out. I had great moves."

"Too bad they don't have a professional dodgeball league now. I bet you could be the Michael Jordan of dodgeball."

"I could," I said. "Anyway, I remember finding it when we went out for recess. The lunchpail. Looked like road kill, peanut butter oozing out the sides. Everybody thought it was funny—all the other kids. You know I still feel bad when I think about it. Forty years ago and I still feel bad. What's with that? It was almost like the lunchpail was a sacred trust I was given, and I somehow failed. Like I got the Holy Grail and then went to sleep and let somebody run it over with a car. I can remember picking it up and walking home. I don't know how I knew where home was, but it couldn't have been very far. . . . Am I crying?"

"Crying is allowed."

"I never cry," I said.

"We'll just call this an exception then."

"Man."

"Go on."

"I was crying then, too. All the way home, just sobbing. Like it was the saddest thing in the world. It was just a lunchpail. I handed it to my mother like it was an offering. Arms outstretched, eyes closed. And my mother cried, too. I remember that."

"And . . . ?"

"Oh," I said. ". . . Just more stuff."

"Talk about it," he said. "The more stuff. It's important."

"Nothing to talk about. My father found the lunchpail and wanted to know what happened and so forth and so on, and I was a wrong-o and a stupid kid and forever after I carried my lunch in a paper sack. A brown paper sack. Never got another lunchpail. Ever. Lunchpails, I learned from those who supposedly knew, were actually for sissies. The big guys always carried their lunches in paper bags. Brown paper bags. And God knows, I wanted to be one of the big guys."

"And be right," said Tyler.

"Sure."

"Did you ever notice that the guys who were right had all the power? Parents. Teachers. Coaches. Priests. Umpires. They were just always right. By definition and title. *I'm the coach and I'm right. I'm a priest and I'm right. God will punish you because I say so.* It's like the divine right of people who are bigger than you are."

"Yeah," I said. "But you know, I still like to be right. There's something about it."

"Most people do," he said. "But it's overrated—being right."

"So here's my question," I said. "Why?"

"Price is way too high."

"What's the price?"

"You have to give up peace, serenity, being a part of . . . Ask yourself a simple question: Would I rather be happy, or would I rather be right? Not always an easy decision. Always being right, always needing to be right, separates me from people. If I'm right, you're obviously wrong. At best different, at worst inferior. Being right means I'm bulletproof. You can't touch me. I'm an emotional Superman. What are you going to say to someone who's always right? Who, no matter what, always has this hammer of righteousness at his side. I'm right—BAM! I'm so right I'm going to hit you over the head with it."

"So being right's not always good?"

"Nothing wrong with being right," he said. "It's the need to be right *all the time* that's deadly. It separates. If I have to be right, what do you have to be?"

"Wrong?" I said.

"That's what people think. Took me years to understand that we could both be right. Remember the old philosophical puzzle about two people looking at the same penny."

"That was probably an upper-division course I never got to."

"Here it is. . . . Two people are looking at the same penny. Number-One Guy is looking directly down on it, and Number-Two Guy is looking at it sort of from the side."

"Which one's the philosopher?" I said.

"I'm ignoring questions that are not pertinent."

"Sorry."

"So Number-One Guy says the penny is round. Is he right?"

"I'm proceeding cautiously," I said. "I'm going to hazard a yes."

"And you are absolutely right," he said. "Bravo. But the Number-Two Guy says, 'No, it's sort of elliptical, more oval than round.' Can he be right, too?"

"Yes?"

"Well, how can that be?" said Tyler, palms open. "The penny can't be round *and* elliptical, can it?"

"I get it," I said. "Of course. Depends on where you are. How you're looking at it. They could both be right."

Tyler lit a cigarette and stared at me through the smoke.

"Could be, Mister Bear. Could just be."

"You get smarter as you get older?" I said.

"Dumber," he said. "When I was your age, I knew everything. Absolutely everything."

"You know, I don't have to be right all the time. Not all the time."

"Good. Being right's not all it's cracked up to be. Neither is being smart."

I took a sip of coffee.

"The coffee's Vienna Roast," I said. "Your favorite."

"You are a prince among men."

"Don't I wish," I said.

"Shakespeare says, *There's nothing either good or bad but thinking makes it so.*"

"You believe that?" I said.

"I think so," he said. "Next week is The Need to Get Even. One of my favorites."

"I'll remember," I said.

"I hope so. Because I may forget."

"No big deal. See you Thursday."

"When?" But he was smiling.

"Good night, Dr. Strangelove. See you soon."

Three

The Need to Get Even

An eye for an eye and soon the whole world's blind.
—Mahatma Gandhi

The Need to Get Even, right?" I said. "That's the one for this week?"

"You got any cigarettes? I forgot mine."

"You quitting again?"

"No," he said. "I just forgot mine."

"Because I know when you quit, first thing you do is quit buying. You forget I'm familiar with the routine, Tyler. You say you quit, then you bum smokes for a week or so and finally admit you're only *trying* to quit, not actually quitting. A test run. But of course by then you're back smoking full time so it doesn't make any difference. At least by that time you're buying your own smokes."

"What would I do without you to define and interpret my motives?"

"You'd probably be lost," I said. "And just think I do this absolutely for free. Your gratitude is more than enough."

"Somehow I think this is far from free," he said. "And the gratitude is negligible. Believe me. Back to the issue at hand. Cigarettes. What did Ann smoke?"

"Something mentholated, I think. Salems maybe."

"Ugh . . ."

"You know, for a supposedly spiritual-type guy, you seem to have a lot of those vices we're all trying to get rid of."

"Why?" he said.

"Why do you have a lot of those vices?"

"No. Why are we all trying to get rid of them?"

"Because . . . Because we're trying to live spiritual lives."

"You can't live a spiritual life and smoke?"

"Well, the idea is that we try to . . ."

"Never mind. We can discuss that next week when we talk about the Need to Look Good. Just let me say this: It's not a well-known fact, but Jesus chewed tobacco."

"Tyler . . . Where do you come up with these things?"

"You'll see. Wait 'til they find the rest of the Dead Sea Scrolls."

"If there's a Judgment Day, you may be in big trouble."

He ignored the comment. Or maybe he didn't hear me. He wears a hearing aid, but sometimes I suspect it's either turned off or he never bothers to put batteries in it.

"Now," he said. "The need to get even. What's all that about? I know you've given it some careful thought."

"We're talking revenge?" I said.

"Not necessarily, though that's often a large part of it.

Think of it at least partially as playing catch-up. Which is what revenge is anyway."

"Catching up to what?"

"Didn't you ever have that feeling that you were running a little behind the pack? That you had to try a little harder just to keep up? That everyone else was cruising along in some middle gear and you were going all out, sweating like a fat moose and not catching up? Maybe not even getting close?"

"I don't remember the part about the fat moose, but I know about trying to catch up, thinking I had to work extra hard just to stay even."

"Same thing," he said. "So what happens if we can't get even, maybe can't even catch up?"

"We . . . lose?" I ventured. I never know where he's going with these things. Truth was, I hadn't given it much thought. A mistake I would not make again.

"Poor, Edward. Really shabby. Hardly worthy of you. Shows a decided lack of thought about the subject at hand."

"Well, I . . ."

"You can do better. What happens to people who have a deep need to get even?"

"I think they . . ."

"And why would someone have that need to start with?"

"One at a time," I said. "I imagine that if the people who *need* to get even actually *do* get even, they'd be okay. I mean if they actually *did* catch up. Get even."

"That's what those guys in the Mafia say just before they shoot you. Nothing personal. Just business . . . *Boom!*"

"Well, tell me what you mean by getting even. Give me an example."

"Okay," he said. "Example number one. You're driving along the freeway; somebody cuts you off and flips you the finger. What's your first impulse?"

"Run him off the road and laugh as his car rolls over and over, crushing him beyond recognition."

"Good healthy impulse. What do you actually do?"

"Depends," I said. "Most of the time, I flip him off and tailgate him for a while. If he's not looking in the rearview mirror, I honk my horn and flip him off again. Be sure he knows how unhappy I am about what he did."

"Make you feel better?"

"Since when have you been into all this feely stuff? I'm not sure if I notice *how* I feel at the moment. And what does feeling have to do with it? First of all, I'm pissed because he cuts me off. Then to add insult to injury, he flips me off. What kind of deal is that? I feel angry, that's how I feel. And if his car bursts into flames, I'll feel happy. Really happy. We can't just let people do things like that."

"Why?"

"Because we . . . we have to . . ."

"Get even?"

"Sure. I mean if people thought they could get away with that, we'd have . . . anarchy," I said. "Complete anarchy. Everybody would be cutting everyone else off, flipping them the bird."

"And getting even makes it better?" he said. "Is that like making more bombs so we can have peace? Or killing people so the world will be safe for democracy?" He looked around the room. "Maybe I *will* have one of those Salems."

I got up and retrieved a pack from the cupboard.

"Think of what would happen," I said, "if there were no laws. If we just let everybody do whatever they wanted to do."

"Why do you keep the cigarettes around?" he asked. "You expect her to come back?"

"You kidding? Man, I'm glad she's gone."

He gave me a funny look.

"*What?*" I said.

"Nothing . . ."

He took a cigarette out of the package and looked at it.

"You suppose if I took the filter off, there would be less of a menthol taste?"

"Can't tell you," I said. "I never smoked menthols."

He snapped the filter off, lit it and made a face.

"Ugh," he said. "Awful . . ."

"Probably a character-building experience."

"A common misconception," he said, picking tobacco off his tongue.

"What is?"

"That because an experience is difficult, it builds character. Much better to learn from joyful experiences. Actually much easier."

"You think?"

"Suffering is only good if it teaches you to stop suffering."

"Can I quote you on that?" I said.

"You may," he said, "though it's not original with me."

"So back to my question," I said. "What if there were no laws?"

"That's not the question."

"Then what is?"

"The question is why do we have the need to get even?"

"It's human nature," I said. "Everybody wants to get even."

"Not true, and there's a part two to the question. What would happen if everyone stopped trying to get even?"

"Like I said—anarchy."

"Remember that person who just cut you off and flipped you the bird?"

"I'm still steamed," I said.

"Suppose you smiled and waved at him . . . using all your fingers?"

"He'd probably think I was some kind of a nutcase. Then he'd go cut somebody else off and give *them* the finger. Guys like that gotta be stopped."

"Maybe smiling and waving at him would get him to stop," said Tyler.

"That doesn't sound even remotely possible."

"Thou shalt not avenge," he said. "You ever hear that?"

"Not unless it was on CNN last week."

"How about, 'Vengeance is mine, saith the Lord. I shall repay.'"

"Then maybe you can get God or the Great Pumpkin or the Force to smile and wave at him," I said. "Use some of that heavy-duty spiritual muscle people say you have."

"That's what I was trying to do," he said.

"No, you were trying to get *me* to smile and . . ."

He got that goofy look on his face that he gets when he thinks he's made his point.

"Oh, no," I said. "No way I'm falling for that Everyone-Is-Divine routine."

"The eye with which you see God is the same eye with which God sees you," he said. "Ever hear that?"

"The Great Pumpkin?"

"Meister Eckhart."

"Who's Meister Eckhart?" I said.

"Third baseman with the Red Sox in the mid-thirties. Before your time. Good glove, no stick."

"Tyler, Tyler." I shook my head.

"He was a mystic. Thirteenth century maybe. Almost burned at the stake as a heretic."

"I can see why."

"You reap what you sow," he said. "What goes out, comes back."

"And a free translation of that would be?"

"What goes around, comes around," he said. "You get what you give. Spiritual calculus. Also penitentiary wisdom."

"That where you learned about getting even?" I said. "The penitentiary?"

"I already knew before I got there. Folsom is where I did my graduate work. I learned from experts, highly skilled practitioners in the art of getting even, people who had elevated it to high art. They knew exactly how much pain and suffering to extract to even the scales. Often only a life would do. And sometimes a life was worth a pack of cigarettes. Or less."

"What's that have to do with the guy on the highway?"

"Everything," said Tyler. "Same process, different venue. The Need to Get Even. The idea that if you don't get even, you're less of a man, less of a person, that you somehow lack the basic ingredients, even the basic skills, that define us as human beings."

"Suppose that guy cuts me off again tomorrow and gives me the finger?" I said.

"Suppose the other guy's a divine messenger?"

I took a deep breath.

"I'm trying to picture Jesus in a BMW. And don't answer a question with a question. Isn't that what you always tell me?"

"Guilty," he said.

"Okay. Suppose that guy cuts me off again tomorrow and gives me the finger?"

"Not likely."

"Could happen," I said. "As I recall, just yesterday I waved and told him to have a nice day. He'll probably be waiting by the roadside so he can cut me off again. Can't wait. I'm a patsy. A pushover. He loves guys like me."

"Possible, but still not likely," he said. "There is an old saying about certain types of people showing up in your life on a regular basis. If you meet one jerk a day, it may be just bad luck. If you meet two, that's cause to wonder. If you're meeting three or more you should perhaps look in the mirror and see if it's not you."

"The jerk, you mean."

"Right," he said.

"I'll give that a qualified maybe."

"So if the guy cuts you off and flips you the bird tomorrow, what are you going to do?" he said. "The new you."

"I'll borrow one of your favorite techniques," I said. "How about right action."

"Bravo, Edward. . . . But what *is* the right action?"

"I'll say, 'Bless you, you jerk,' and wave with all my fingers."

"Well done," said Tyler.

"But my heart won't be in it."

"Not necessary that your heart be in it. That will come later. For now all that is required is right action. Very Buddhist. You might even say a prayer for him."

"Don't push it, Tyler. It's all I can do to keep from running him off the road."

"You know what Gandhi says about violence?"

"No."

"An eye for an eye and soon the whole world's blind."

"But I don't see how all that right action crap is going to make anything different. I still think the guy's a jerk. I still want to run him off the road and watch his car burn. Preferably with him inside. Barring that, I hope he dies from some lingering painful disease."

"The difference is that you don't *act* that way," said Tyler. "You've heard that old saying about *fake it 'til you make it.* Or *act as if and pretty soon it won't be an act anymore.*"

"Yeah."

"Same deal. Bring the body, take the right action, the mind and spirit will soon follow."

"I don't know if I'm ready for that," I said. "Sounds a little too spiritual for me."

"If you wait 'til you're ready, you'll never do it. As the Nike commercial says, *Just do it.*"

"Just stop getting even?"

"Yes."

"What will happen if I do?"

"What will happen if you don't?" he said.

"We're not doing the question-question thing," I reminded him.

"Right. Okay then, what will happen if you *don't*, is that the guy in the Chevy pickup or the Ford Taurus, or worse yet, the BMW, will keep showing up in your life, keep cutting you off, and giving you the bird. It's called a Lesson."

"That's the payoff?"

"You want a payoff?" he said.

"Not necessarily."

"Be honest."

"Okay. I want a payoff."

"The payoff is that pretty soon you won't need to get even anymore."

"That's a payoff?" I said. "A big prize? I won't need to get even anymore? This is a big deal?"

"It's a much bigger deal than you might think. It will literally change your life. Remember the phrase, *We ceased fighting everything and everyone*? You've probably read it a hundred times. It's like that. But you have to stop trying to get even before you find out what that phrase really means. First the action, then the result. That's the way it works. Not the other way around. Action, result. Action, result."

"Like the horse, then the cart," I said. "Horse, then the cart. Like that?"

"You got it."

"Sounds simple when you say it."

"Words can be deceptive," he said. "Simple and easy are not the same thing." He stubbed his cigarette out in the ashtray. "God, they're awful."

"Could I lay in a supply of Marlboros for your visit next week?"

"Very possible that I won't be smoking at all next week. Very possible. Hate to have you waste money."

"I'll take the chance," I said.

"So . . . recapping our discussion, Edward. Can we agree that the scales of justice probably never get perfectly balanced? At least in this life. That there's really no such thing as getting even? That the *need* to get even is much more destructive than we first realized?"

"I think I can agree with that."

"That if anger and violence and impatience go out, that's what comes back?"

"Right."

"I love to be right," he said.

"But do you *need* to be right?" I countered.

He smiled.

"Not as often as I did," he said. "Progress, not perfection . . . 'Til next week?"

"I'll be here. The Need to Look Good?"

"Ah, yes," he said. "The Need to Look Good. Almost cost me my life."

"How?"

"Tune in next week."

Four

The Need to Look Good

I'd rather look good than eat.
—Anonymous

W hen were you born?"
"The fifties."

"The fifties," he said, staring at something off to my left. "I was in big trouble in the fifties."

"And I was just a baby."

"Hardly seems possible."

"What? That you were in big trouble or that I was just a baby?"

"You missed the sixties?"

"Not entirely."

"I was in big trouble for some of the sixties, too."

"Maybe you were just a troubled guy," I said.

He smiled and looked at me.

"I like that," he said. "Lots better than what the judge said."

"What did the judge say?"

"As I remember, it was something very uncomplimentary. But, I digress. The subject for this evening—the need to look good. So, what's the deal with this need?"

"Perfectly normal," I said. "Everybody has this . . . desire at least to look good."

"Desire or need?" he said.

"Semantics," I said.

"Now you sound like me."

"God forbid."

"You should be so lucky," he said.

"After some consideration," I said, "careful consideration I might add, I've come to the conclusion that everyone actually *needs* to look good. It's another one of those built-in things."

"Like instincts? Like bees and honey, birds and flying?"

"Yeah," I said. "Like that."

"You don't think it's learned then?"

"Well . . ." I hate it when he does that. He begins these verbal maneuvers until he has you trapped in a corner and you end up saying things you don't mean to say. "Not necessarily."

"So maybe it's a little instinctual and a little learned," he said. "Like a combination. Half-instinct and half-learned. A half-and-half thing. Like that milk stuff you buy at the market."

"I know what you're doing, Tyler," I said. "You're not fooling me for a minute, hiding behind all that semantics bullshit. You're just going to shove the words around until they come out like you want them to come out. And I'll end up looking like some kind of a dummy."

He gave me that innocent shrug like, *Who, me?*

"You'll look bad, Edward?"

"Never mind about that."

"I'm just after the truth," he said. "Or whatever we can know of the truth."

"Do you honestly feel that anyone wants to look *bad*?" I said. "Anyone? Of course everyone wants to look good. Needs to look good even. It's human nature."

"You know the difference between wants and needs?"

"Yes, I know the difference between wants and needs. Jesus . . ." I must admit to a little impatience here. Tyler can be very irritating at times. "Don't you?"

"Is it possible you're getting a little testy?" he said. "Do I detect some impatience here?"

"Jesus, Tyler, sometimes . . . Man . . ."

"Very simple. Don't complicate it. Just breathe. And tell me the difference between wants and needs."

I took a deep breath.

"Okay. A want is something you'd *like* to have. Desire to have. Not necessarily something you have to have. Like I want an ice cream cone, but I'm not going to die if I don't get one. Now a need is something that you *do* have to have, without which you're not going to make it. Something essential."

"Food?" he said.

"Sure."

"Shelter?"

"Yeah," I said.

"Anything else? Sex, maybe?"

"If we didn't have sex, we wouldn't have people, Tyler. That's got to be one of the needs."

"Let me play devil's advocate," he said. "Let's say we've already got plenty of people. Too many people. Now we can even clone people. Maybe we don't need sex."

"Sex is an essential part of living."

"Essential?" he said.

"Must have been essential *once*," I said. "I mean how did all this get started? You think Adam and Eve smuggled a copy of *The Joy of Sex* into the Garden of Eden so they could learn how to jump-start the human race? This is the missionary position. Time to practice."

"I can hardly believe you just said that."

"I can play it back on the tape if you want."

"That won't be necessary," he said.

"How old are you?"

"Not as old as Adam or Eve, but almost."

"Come on," I said. "How old?"

"You know what Satchel Paige said about age?"

"No," I said. "Just tell me and get it over with."

"He said, *How old would you be if you didn't know how old you was?*"

"I don't get it."

"Well, I suppose there's only so much information you can get out of a library. Then again maybe you're not old enough."

"So how old are you?"

"Still on the good side of seventy," he said.

"Then you may not need sex."

"Why would you think that?"

"Because you just said you didn't think sex was necessary. Or essential."

"I *asked* if it was essential. Asked. A question."

"Implied," I said.

"Asked," he said.

"And you're seventy years old."

"In a few years," he said. "And what's that got to do with it?"

"Okay, you're almost seventy," I said. "Being seventy probably has a lot to do with it."

"Actually, Edward, I . . . Well, you'll just have to wait and find out for yourself. Age brings a certain mystical dimension to sex."

"Like air guitar for retirees."

"That's very funny," he said. "Inaccurate, but funny. And mystical is perhaps a poor translation of what actually happens; you almost have to have the experience. You probably think that sex is more important when you're younger."

"I *do* think that."

"It's not true," he said. "Take it from somebody who's been both young *and* old."

"So I have something to look forward to?"

"As long as you're breathing in and out, you have something to look forward to."

"Jesus, Tyler, you always . . ."

"I'm just trying to establish some framework for our discussion. Truth is, our needs are very few; our wants tend to get out of hand. Especially those of us in the recovery community. We, myself included, want to look good. *Need* to look good. At all times. Under all circumstances. We labor under this illusion that if we *look* well, we *are* well. Here's another favorite of mine: If enough people *think* I'm well, I must be well. By definition. By acclamation maybe. And the more people think that, the weller I get."

"And you're telling me this because you think I'm like that. You think I'm shallow like that."

"Nobody said anything about shallow. Did I say shallow? I'm merely asking you to consider the possibility that the need to look good is a major factor in your life."

"I'm not concerned with what people think about me, Tyler."

"You're oblivious to what people think of you?"

"Well," I said. "Maybe not oblivious, but at least I'm not obsessed with it."

"Aren't you the guy who wouldn't go to the Fulmer Street Meeting last week because you had that cold sore on your lip?"

"There are tons of women at the Fulmer Street Meeting, Tyler. You know that. And that was a big, ugly cold sore. I didn't want to go looking like some kind of leper. A small cold sore, I might have gone."

"You didn't seem to mind when we were at Burger King," he said.

"That's different."

"You wanted to look good?" he said. "For the ladies."

"Everybody wants to look good, Tyler. That's not a big revelation."

"You *needed* to look good?"

"Well . . ."

"That's what I would have done not too many years ago."

"What?"

"I'd have stayed away because I had an unsightly zit on my face."

"It's not a zit," I said. "It's a cold sore. I had zits when I was a kid. Lots of zits. I ever tell you that?"

"No."

"They used to call me pizza face."

"Aren't kids wonderful?" he said. "Someone told me that sores like that, cold sores, were supposed to be some form of herpes. You ever hear that?"

"Goddamit, Tyler, I don't have herpes."

"I didn't say you had herpes," he said.

"You implied that I did."

"Well, whatever it was, I'd have stayed away because I wouldn't have looked my best. God forbid. Every blemish that crept into view on the sallow landscape of my already-ravaged face became another reason to hide. Sometimes a reason to die. And I already had plenty of those. I'd have stayed home and *thought* about it—about the pimples and the zits and the fact that, as my mother had always suspected, I wasn't very diligent about washing my face. What a bad combination—me and my head alone at night. Ugh! What I failed to realize was that nearly everyone else was also self-obsessed and most likely wouldn't have noticed.

"But there was a time, Edward, when looking good was more important than eating. Than living even. Times when I literally put my life on the line so I could look good, so people would think that I was fearless, bulletproof, faster than a speeding bullet *and* able to leap tall buildings in a single bound. *Man, he'll do anything.* That's what they said. Fact is, I was *so* terrified, I would have done anything to convince you I *wasn't* afraid."

"You afraid? This I'd have liked to see."

"Sure, I came into this process without an identifiable Self. No infrastructure. I was what people thought I was. I lived in other people's minds. I was a reflection of their opinions. An emotional moon spinning out of control across some endless, terrifying night sky. And if you thought I was okay, I was okay. If *everyone* thought I was okay, then I was *really* okay. See how it works? I had a *need* to look good. That's the only way I could tell anything about myself."

"Doesn't seem like a smart way to live."

"Maybe not," he said. "But if that's all you've got for openers, that's where you start. Recognizing it helps."

"So is it really so awful? This need to look good? I mean don't lots of people have it?"

"Of course. That's why the cosmetics industry is a multi–billion-dollar industry. Trouble is, the message is that if you *look* okay, you *are* okay."

"Not such a good message."

"I suppose if everybody was pretty, if everybody had money and nobody ever got old or wrinkly or sick, it wouldn't be so bad."

"I'm still young and pretty," I said.

"Indeed you are," he said.

"And you, though certainly old and wrinkly, are not all that bad looking. And you've managed somehow to look wise. God knows how something like that could have happened."

"We can chalk it up to luck. And I'd rather be lucky than almost anything else."

"You always say that," I said.

"Because it's true."

"So you think this need to look good is actually deadly?"

"Indeed. It would have us believe that life works from the outside in, not the other way around. A Chinese proverb says, *That which enters from the outside, can never become your own real treasure.* If I believe that life works from the outside in, I will always be at the mercy of something external—looks, money, power, prestige, image—all of it. Actually, and this is very important, Edward . . ."

"I'm listening," I said.

"Actually, life works from the inside out. Turns out to be an inside job after all. You remember that."

"I do."

"And speaking of living from the inside out, how is your interior life?"

"Okay, I guess."

"You ever need to look so good that you can't talk about what's eating your lunch?"

"Sometimes," I said. I always have to hedge a little until I find out where he's headed.

"You know if I need to look so good that I can't tell anyone about my fears, my struggles, my doubts, my insanity, if nobody ever tells anybody, we're all going to feel like we're the only ones that have them—the struggles and the heartaches. And we're not going to be able to recover. Any of us. We'll all go to those meetings and everyone, because they have this terrible *need* to look good, will say, *I'm fine. How are you? Oh, I'm fine, too. My kids are sick and my brother died, but I'm fine. Me, too. Wow, my mother just died, but I'm okay because I know she's in a better place. . . . Me, too. I'm fine, I'm fine. I'm . . . dying because I can't go on living like this anymore.* We'll be so into looking good and being okay that a month from now everybody will be drunk or high or suicidal or eating jelly donuts at midnight or out searching in one more dark night for some sequestered grave in which to bury our dreams.

"You see it only works if we can somehow get over this terrible need to look good all the time and actually tell someone, some other person, at the risk of perhaps looking bad, maybe tell a whole roomful of other persons, about how we're not doing so terribly well at the moment, about some things that have happened that were not particularly joyful, that perhaps we have *done* some things that we are not especially proud of, and we need to share those things, to bring them out into the light before they kill us."

"You think I should have gone to the meeting anyway. Cold sore and all?"

"You think nobody will like you if you've got a zit on your lip?"

"Hey, no questions to answer questions," I said.

"Sorry."

"The answer is no, but it looks absolutely awful, Tyler."

"I thought you didn't care what people thought about you?"

"Well, about some things maybe . . ."

"You see, looking good is not necessarily about clothes, your appearance, zits, what kind of car you drive, what

woman you have on your arm or whether you've got chili
stains on your shirt."

"Okay. What *is* it about?"

"The need to look good encompasses everything. It's just
as often the pretense of appearing to be okay and oh-so-well-
adjusted in the face of some terrible adversity. *See me, Lois?
I'm bulletproof. Nothing can hurt me. Bullets and feelings
bounce right off me.* You've heard the line that says, *I'm as
sick as I am secretive?* Or, *Admit your faults to Him and to
your fellows?*"

"I have."

"What do you think that's about?" he said.

"What's admitting my faults about?"

"Yeah. And being as sick as my secrets."

"It's about having to look good at all costs."

"Bravo! Who's your boss at Safeway? I'm going to call and
tell him how smart you are."

"I don't think he'll be impressed," I said.

"And if we're all so busy looking good, it's guaranteed to
keep us isolated. From life. From each other. From our-
selves. Remember the *we* thing? *We* admitted *we* were
powerless over whatever-it-is. To get over the tyranny of
looking good, I have to take the terrible risk of letting others
see me when I'm not at my best, when I may feel very fool-
ish and vulnerable. I've got to raise my hand and say, *Here I
am, warts and all. My message is that it's possible to recover
from my various addictions and not look good.* I once heard
a guy say that, *I came here to save my ass and found out it
was attached to my soul.*"

"Interesting concept," I said.

"Perhaps a little crude, but nonetheless accurate," he said. "Remember what Winnie-the-Pooh said: *At times the bravest knight, may find his armor much too tight.*"

"And I know one from the Zen world," I said.

"I'm holding my breath."

"Very bad," I said. "Always remember to breathe. Isn't that what you always tell me?"

"The saying?"

"Shiver when it's cold, sweat when it's hot . . ."

"Sage advice," he said. "Be where you are. So how are you Edward? Really."

"I'm . . . I'm actually not doing terribly well."

"Ah-h-h-h . . . We have lessons to deal with?"

"A few problems," I said.

"There are only lessons," he said.

"There is Pamela, of course. Pamela and then my boss Daniel Ohlmeyer at work."

"Sweet Pamela Parsons," he said. "Plus Danny Boy. Your cup overfloweth."

"She's a load sometimes, Tyler," I said.

"And you, of course, are light as a feather, agreeable, compliant, loving and true."

"This may surprise you, but I'm not always that way."

"You remember what the next deadly need is?" he said.

"Give me a hint."

"Coming up only one short week from today is the Need to Judge."

"The need to judge."

"And apparently just in the nick of time," he said.

"You think I . . ."

"Oh, we all do," he said, abruptly getting up from the table. "I have to go do my laundry."

"At eight o'clock at night?"

"I do some of my best laundry at night."

"Of course," I said. "I should have known. You and Count Dracula. The night-shift guys."

Five

The Need to Judge

Do not judge your neighbor until you have walked two moons in his moccasins.
—Northern Cheyenne Saying

D id you have a nice day?" asked Tyler.

"No, Tyler," I said. "I had a terrible goddam day. A hopelessly horseshit day."

"Don't hold back now," he said. "Tell me how you really feel."

"God . . . You know how many lunatics come through the checkout line at Safeway on an average day?"

"I can't guess," he said. "Dozens?"

"Hundreds possibly. Lunatics and . . . criminals for chrissakes."

"Careful about the criminals," he said. "You know how sensitive I am about that."

"Jesus, God. There are people out there, Tyler, who are useless. Worse than useless."

"Just taking up space."

"Right."

"Bottom feeders," he said. "Mouth breathers."

"Yeah."

"You've judged them and found them wanting?"

"You could say that. There are people out there who enjoy being unpleasant. Actually enjoy it. Get their kicks that way."

"I wonder why?"

"God knows."

"They're out to get you?"

"Oh, it's not just me," I said. "Not by a long shot. In case you think I've slipped into self-pity. Ask any bus driver, waitress or bellhop. Jerks, Tyler. That's what I see. As far as the eye can see—jerks."

"You want some coffee?" he said.

"I haven't made it yet. I just got home, for chrissakes. How do you expect me to . . ."

"I'll make it," he said.

"Man . . . I feel like I've been run over by a truck."

"The Reality Truck," he said cheerfully.

"The Reality Truck. You and your Reality Truck."

"And the train," he said. "Don't forget about the Reality Train."

"How could I forget the Train? That's all you talked about when we first met. *The Reality Train is leaving, Edward. You getting aboard or just going to sit there at the station and watch?*"

"That was about action," he said. "Doing something. All abo-o-o-ard."

"Spare me tonight. . . . The coffee's in the cupboard."

"I know," he said. "If you recall, I've done this before. Just sit and tell me about all the unworthy people you met today."

"Tyler, Tyler. . . . You wouldn't believe it."

"Try me," he said.

"I'll get to it. . . . You know, for some reason I've been thinking about your father lately. Was he really such a jerk?"

"You want the French Roast Fine Grind Gourmet Coffee or the Irish Creme?"

"Let's go with the Irish Creme," I said. "I don't feel very French Roast tonight."

"Irish Creme it is—the Drinking Man's Coffee. And remember that we're actually drinking gourmet coffee instead of warm brown liquid at the Mission. That fact alone might be cause for celebration. . . . As for my father, he was a drunk. That explains his behavior; it doesn't excuse it. Died of cirrhosis. I told you about it."

"I remember. The back room."

"Yeah," he said. "Was he a jerk? I thought so for a long time, but now I just don't know."

"My father is."

"What started you thinking about all this? Fathers and sons?"

"Maybe all the useless people that showed up today."

"You're sure?" he said. "I mean about your father?"

"Yeah," I said. "I'm sure."

"When are you going to make peace with that?"

"I don't know."

"As a suggestion," he said, "don't wait."

"Don't wait? Aren't you the guy who told me it took you

twenty-nine years before you finally resolved it? Twenty-nine years and twenty-nine letters, for chrissakes?"

"I don't advocate the delay. Your dad's still alive?"

"If you can call it living. He exists in a small trailer over in Echo Park. Alone, of course. He's run everybody out of his life."

"Then don't wait," he said. "It's much easier when they're alive."

"I . . . I don't like him, Tyler," I said. "I may even hate him."

"Not relevant," he said.

"How do you make peace with someone you hate?"

"Like everything else. You just do it."

"You think it's normal to hate your own father?"

"What do I know about normal?" said Tyler. "You should ask somebody who's got a better grip on things like that. What I *do* know is that it's probably not healthy."

"You mean not healthy for me," I said.

"Right. For you. I don't think hate's healthy for anyone."

"Down with hate."

"You've judged him and found him wanting. That's bad if you discover it in other people, worse if it happens to be your father. Or your mother. They were your first deities. Powerful beings who brought you sustenance, warmth, love. Then one day we discover that they're only human after all. Bigger, but just human. We often find that hard to forgive. The greater the expectation, the greater the disappointment. Worse than that, they may even be absolute jerks."

"Absolutely."

"Then what?" he said.

"What do you mean, then what?"

"I mean what do you do about it?"

"I can't *do* anything about it, Tyler. They're either jerks or they're not."

"What does the Serenity Prayer say?"

"You know what the Serenity Prayer says. You don't need me to tell you."

"I need you to remind yourself," he said. "First part: *God grant me the serenity to accept the things I cannot change.* Can you change your father?"

"No. Not likely."

"Very perceptive of you. . . . You take anything in your coffee?"

"Just black," I said. "You know that."

"I forget sometimes."

"Did I ever tell you I have this secret fantasy about taking a . . . certain kind of woman to bed."

"Are we allowed to say what kind?" said Tyler.

"A prostitute."

"Ahhhh," he said. "I see."

"Doesn't that seem weird?"

"No."

"You ever do that?" I said.

"Have a fantasy like that?" he said.

"No, no. I mean actually do that."

"I have," he said.

"Recently?"

"Depends on what you mean by recently."

"Tyler. God. Sometimes I don't know about you. How was it?"

He shook his head and smiled.

"As I recall, there were some elements of perfection to it."

"You know, all my experiences with women haven't been terrific, Tyler."

"Old Chinese proverb says, *You learn to stand by falling down.*"

"Bless the Chinese."

"And, you may have forgotten some of the parts that make up the experience. There's the sharing part. Despite what we may think, it's not actually a solo performance. Then there's the basic position."

"What's that?"

"Gratitude."

"Don't tell me," I said. "That's the position just after the missionary position?"

"Just before."

"Of course. Before."

"What brings up all *this* stuff?" he said.

"I don't know," I said.

"Judgment?"

"Maybe. Sometimes I think I'm just crazy. That I've always been crazy, and there's absolutely no chance it will ever change. You ever think that? I mean about yourself?"

"Yeah. Fortunately, crazy is not normally a criminal offense," he said. "Let's leave all that for a later discussion. Here's your coffee. . . . So why this need to judge your father?"

"I don't know if I need to judge him. It just happens that way. I formed an opinion about him. It just didn't happen to be very good. But don't we all judge others? I mean, isn't that normal?"

"What's the opposite of judging?" he said.

"Uh . . .The opposite of judging is . . . loving?"

"How do you do with loving the people in the checkout line at Safeway?"

"I don't think I'm there yet."

"How about if the opposite of judging was accepting?" he said.

"I could maybe do better with that. Maybe."

"So you could possibly accept the people going through the checkout line? Some of the people anyway."

"I could try. But Tyler, they're such turkeys."

"They're different?"

"Right, they're different. They smell bad, half of them. I mean *really* bad. They use food stamps to buy soda pop and jelly donuts instead of real food for chrissakes. Then there's . . ."

"Are they different colors?" he said.

"Different than what?"

"Different than the color you are?"

"Tyler . . ."

"You know that's what we have wars about. Think about it. We find people who are different than we are. . . . Different color, different religion, different-looking, people who talk funny. We find them, and we judge them—and then we kill them. That's what Manifest Destiny is all about. Doing God's work. Makes us feel better. Safer, and God knows we want to feel safe. At last the *others* are all gone and there's only us, the chosen ones, people who look the same and talk the same language. Obviously the 'right' kind of folks. I feel better already just thinking about it. And the way we know they're different is that we judge them, find them inferior because they don't share our skin color and our values and our special God, we render a decision, we pass sentence, then poof, we make them disappear."

"They steal things."

"Horrors! First it's food stamps and now we have hungry people trying to steal food. Sweet Jesus, what next?"

"Sure, make fun," I said. "You're not the one working there. I have a responsibility to . . ."

"Why do you think we judge people?"

"So we'll . . . I mean there's nothing wrong with judging people, Tyler. We judge things all the time. . . .The weather, the traffic, the state of the nation, the condition of your car . . ."

"Maybe we judge people so we can decide things about them. Separate ourselves from them. Thumbs up or thumbs down. Guilty or innocent. Judging the state of the weather or the condition of your car is a lot less complicated."

"So you think the opposite of judging is accepting?"

"You know the part of the Big Book that says all that stuff about acceptance?"

"Page 449," I said.

"I knew that," he said.

"Everybody knows that."

"That's the part that says: *And acceptance is the answer to all my problems. When I am disturbed, it is because I find some person, place, thing or situation—some fact of my life—unacceptable to me and I can find no serenity until I accept that person, place, thing or situation as being exactly the way it is supposed to be at this moment. Nothing, absolutely nothing happens in God's world by mistake.*"

"For a guy with a lousy memory, you do okay."

"I have trouble with the days of the week," he said.

"Just keep at it," I said. "Keep a notebook. A Daytimer. So you believe that about acceptance being the answer to all my problems?"

"I believe I need to accept the things I can't change. I believe that. Then there's the courage to change the things I can. And of course the final wish—the wisdom to know the difference. Often the tough one."

"I thought this was about the need to judge?" I said.

"It is. The Serenity Prayer is one of the antidotes to the need to judge."

"Which we have decided is deadly?"

"Definitely. Another need that isolates. Therefore deadly. It's odd maybe, but we rarely judge the good in people. Most often our judgments are critical. Give me a quick thumbnail sketch of Sweet Pamela Parsons."

"Selfish, self-centered, ego-driven."

"See?" he said.

"But that's the way she is," I said.

"You find what you look for. Ever hear that?"

"Not until just now."

"The Third Patriarch of Zen says that, *The woodpecker looks for dead branches among the cherry blossoms in bloom.* What do you think he finds?"

"Might be a she, Tyler. Not all woodpeckers are male. Don't be fooled by the name."

"Jesus. You've been spending way too much time in the library. I'll use the editorial, generic *he*. What do you think *he* finds?"

"Dead branches?"

"Well done," he said. " And why doesn't he see the cherry blossoms?"

"Because he's not looking for them?"

"One more right answer, and we'll have you on *Jeopardy*."

"This sounds suspiciously like some of your comic-strip philosophy," I said. "Perhaps something out of the Great Pumpkin Platitudes?"

"What are the two most important spiritual practices?"

"God . . . I don't know, Tyler. How in the world would I know that?"

"Who's got the bad memory now?" he said. "Didn't we just talk about this a few weeks ago?"

"I don't think so. You may have been secretly communing with the Great Pumpkin. I mean, instead of talking to me."

"Maybe it was a few months ago. I don't know what happens to the time."

"And maybe you were talking to someone else," I said.

"I'll accept that as a possibility," he said. "Remote, perhaps, but still a possibility. Anyway, the two most important spiritual practices are gratitude and forgiveness."

"I knew that."

"In a pig's eye you knew that."

"Given enough time I could have come up with it. And what do they have to do with judgments?"

"If your attitude is one of gratitude and forgiveness, there's almost no way you can be judgmental."

"I'm grateful and forgiving," I said.

"Are you grateful for Sweet Pamela?" he said.

"Well, not right this minute."

"Daniel Ohlmeyer?"

"Not terribly," I said. "This is very unfair, Tyler. You pick the two people I'm really struggling with and ask a question like that. I mean probably no one's grateful and forgiving all the time. Not even you, for chrissakes."

"Of course not me," he said. "I'm in the judgment business far more than I'd like to be. I judge the way people drive, what they look like, how they talk, how greedy I think they are. I'm terrible about stuff like that. Perhaps worst of all, I judge myself in the worst possible light. Always."

"So you don't have any room to talk," I said.

"I'm not trying to put myself above the fray, Edward. These Seven Deadly Needs are mine, too. That's how I know about them. Not past tense. How *I know* about them. Today. Now. I still have all of them to varying degrees. It's just that I've come to realize how deadly they are, and how they keep us separated from each other. And what separates us, what gives us that feeling of terminal uniqueness, is what eventually will destroy us."

"So you have not yet arrived at some pinnacle of spiritual awareness?"

"Hardly. It's about progress, not perfection."

"I remember."

"It's very likely that I will go to my grave as a deeply flawed human being," he said.

"My hero."

"And there's no arriving. You know that. There's only the journey."

"Trudging the Road."

"Indeed. . . . Well, enough for one evening?"

"Yeah. You know I meant to ask you last week: Where do

you do your laundry that time of night? Remember you said you were going to do your laundry after you left here?"

"Snow White," he said.

"Over on Belmont? Every drug addict in town does his laundry at Snow White."

"I know."

"Then how come you go there?"

"I think of it as part of my education. Someday I may write a book."

"About what?" I said.

"About all the drug addicts and alcoholics and crazy people I know who do their laundry at night."

"You think anybody wants to read that stuff?"

"I think a lot of drug addicts and alcoholics and crazy people will."

"How many can there be?"

"Oh, lots more than you think, Edward. Lots more. Next week? The Need to Keep Score."

"I'll be ready."

"In the meantime, you might try working on your attitude."

"What's wrong with my goddam attitude?"

"Want me to play the tape back?" he said.

"Never mind."

"Here's what the Dalai Lama says: *A negative attitude benefits no one.*"

"Good night, Tyler."

"Good night, Edward."

Six

The Need to Keep Score

If winning's not important, why do we keep score?

—Anonymous

What's the score?" said Tyler.

"Of what?"

"The game."

"*What* game, for chrissakes?"

"There's only one game on, Edward. That's the Rockies' game."

"The Rockies' game," I said. "Nobody cares about the Rockies, Tyler."

"Wrong," he said. "Lots of people care about the Rockies. And lots of people care about what the score is. Did you work on your attitude this week?"

"Not terribly hard," I said. "I had lots of other things to do."

"You may be wondering how I knew that," he said.

81

"I have a job, Tyler. I spent most of my time at Safeway. Some people don't have jobs."

"You mad at me because I don't have a job?"

"No. I understand that you're very old, and we are far too humane in this country to force the elderly to work."

"You meet lots of nice people at Safeway this week?"

"Some."

"At Safeway?" he said. "How could that be?"

"I want you to know that I actually hate it when you're right. Even partially right."

"And I, of course, love it. Tell the Old Person how it came to pass."

"It's that stuff about you get what you look for. Or what the Dalai Lama said about a negative attitude benefiting no one."

"Go on."

"You know that thing you used to tell me about trying to see a Higher Power in other people? Like saying under my breath, *God lives in you, God lives in you* . . . to everyone I passed on the street. Remember that?"

"Oh, I do," he said. "One of my very best suggestions, by the way."

"It may actually work."

"A major surprise," he said. "You doubted that it would?"

"Let's put it this way: I was uncertain about it."

"You thought I lied?"

"No, Tyler, I didn't think you lied. Not outright. But you've been mistaken before, haven't you? I mean perhaps a chance miscalculation, an error in . . ."

"Tell me how it worked. The suggestion . . ."

"I don't know *how* it worked, but for some reason, after I'd been doing it for a while, saying *God lives in you* to all those jerks in the checkout line, I discovered that I wasn't angry at them. Or I wasn't *as* angry. It's not like they don't still piss me off, but it was somehow different."

"Ah, different," he said. "How so?"

Right about this point in any conversation, Tyler can become especially irritating. He has to keep digging all the time.

"Just . . . I don't know. Just different. Can't we leave it at that? I don't have answers to all those kinds of questions."

"Are you keeping score?"

"Of what?"

"Of how many times you win and how many times you lose?"

"No, I'm not keeping score, Tyler. Whatever that means."

"Everybody keeps score, Edward. I have this secret place in my brain that keeps track of everything. Keeps score so I'll know if I'm ahead or behind."

"And why does it do that, Master?"

"It keeps score so I'll know who's winning and who's not. Or who's winning and who's losing. You want to be a loser?"

"Nobody wants to be a loser, Tyler."

"So how do you know if you're winning or losing unless you keep score?"

"You think I do that? Keep track of everything that happens? Keep score?"

"Remember what we talked about in the need to get even? The guy that cut you off on the freeway?"

"Another jerk," I said. "I remember that guy. Greasy hair

and itty-bitty eyes. BB eyes. Driving a BMW. I still hate him, and he's not even a real person."

"What if you could get ahead and cut *him* off?"

"Great idea."

"Make you feel better?" he said.

Another trap, I thought, but it was too late.

"Maybe."

"The truth," he said.

"Sure, it would make me feel better."

"And since you got even by cutting him off, the score would be . . . ?"

"One to one," I said. "Even up."

"Right. All that time in the checkout line adding up those numbers has not been wasted. You'd be even. No need to retaliate."

"So? I have no idea what you're getting at."

"How would you know when you're even if you don't keep score?"

"Now I'm sorry I asked."

"Why are you always angry at Daniel Ohlmeyer?"

"I'm not always angry at Daniel," I said.

"But most of the time?"

"At least some of the time."

"Why?" he said.

"You want a list?"

"Sure."

"Okay. He embarrasses me in public, actually criticizes me in front of other people. He's arrogant, self-centered, egotistical, and cheap beyond imagining. And those are just for openers."

"What's the score?" he said.

"Between me and Daniel?"

"Yeah."

"I don't know what it is," I said, "but he's way ahead."

"You're losing?"

"Not even close," I said. "On the good days I don't lose too much ground, on the bad days it seems like I'm in full retreat."

"And you know this because you . . . ?"

"You want me to say I know this because I keep score. Right?"

"I don't want you to say anything," he said. "Just tell me how you know."

"Okay, okay. I keep score. You satisfied?"

"Do we need an attitude adjustment break, Edward? Too many questions to deal with. Too much . . ."

"Too much bullshit, Tyler. I mean this doesn't have anything to do with anything. Semantics. Words. Bullshit."

"*Au contraire,* Number-One Pupil. *Au contraire.* It has a great deal to do with everything. And why, you might ask? And *why* you might ask? And why . . ."

"Okay, why? Jesus . . ."

"Because if you're anything like the rest of us, you spend a lot of time taking your emotional pulse, wondering how you're doing, where you are in relation to everyone else. Remember just two or three needs ago we discussed the need to get even? Doesn't necessarily have to be a conscious process, this scorekeeping mechanism, but in some shadowy part of your brain, maybe the reptilian brain, there's a part that wants to make sure you don't fall too far behind. It's like a gyroscope. Tries to keep everything in balance. It hates to lose. Worse than anything, it hates to lose. It feels diminished if it's losing. Afraid. Off-balance. it may even feel like it's going to die."

"Serious business," I said.

"Serious indeed," he said. "Now the crucial question: What would happen if you discovered you were ten points behind in the Life Game and had very little chance of catching up? Ever. Would you think about it a lot? About how far behind you were and how hopeless the situation was? Would you dwell on it? Be afraid?"

Tyler looks so sincere when he asks those questions, but I always feel that there's something deep inside him that's chuckling about the whole thing. It's almost as if he has some kind of second sight that allows him to see behind the landscape we're both looking at.

"No hope of catching up?"

"Not a glimmer."

"Is there a ball in the Life Game?"

"There is indeed," he said.

"Then it's easy. I grab the ball and run. Go home so we can't finish the game and I can't lose."

"Good thinking," he said. "What did Vince Lombardi say about winning?"

"It's not life or death; it's much more important than that."

"Right. So what happens if you don't win?"

"You lose? You die maybe."

"What if I suggested that it wasn't about keeping score or winning or losing, because nobody loses. It's actually impossible to lose. The only way it's even remotely possible to come close to losing is if you refuse to participate. That's it. No losers here in the Life Game. None."

"I'm sure you're aware that there have been some pretty gruesome folks involved in the Life Game, Tyler. I mean you don't have to be Einstein to come up with half a dozen real losers in just the last fifty, sixty years."

"Possibly people who had a great deal to learn," he said. "And to teach. Somebody once said that having wars will eventually teach us not to have wars anymore."

"The old trial and error routine."

"I think that's the one," he said.

"But think of all the people who died while those other people were learning through the trial and error method."

"Nobody dies," he said.

The way he said it, I had the feeling that he thought it was obvious. Like *Nobody dies, dummy. Everybody knows that.* And of course it was not obvious. At all.

"Nobody dies, eh?"

"Nope."

"And nobody loses?"

"No-body," he said.

"Then why *do* we keep score? Why does anybody?"

"It helps maintain the illusion," he said.

"The illusion of what?"

"The illusion that winning or losing is really important. That the world we see is all there is. It's all just beautiful camouflage, Edward. But if we didn't believe it was real, if we didn't have all those cherished illusions, how would we ever learn the lessons?"

"What lessons, for chrissakes?"

"The lessons in Life School," he said.

"Oh, sure. Life School. Which is of course where we learn about the Life Game." He is sometimes at his most exasperating when he gets into his Teacher's Mode.

"You remember," he said. "The lessons. The basics."

"I remember the two most important spiritual practices."

"And just what might they be?"

"Gratitude and forgiveness," I said. "You probably didn't think I remembered, eh?"

"Bravo. There was never a doubt—you're one of my star pupils. We may now be ready for the Double Jeopardy round. Now for the next question," he said. "This is a fill-in-the-blank question. Life is a series of . . ."

"Yes."

"Yes what?"

"Life is a series of blanks."

"Error, Noble Student. Didn't we go over this a few weeks ago?"

"About life being a series of . . . something?"

"Yeah," he said.

"I'm drawing a blank," I said.

"Ha, ha, ha, . . . I'll fill you in—life is a series of surrenders."

"I knew that," I said.

"Unlikely. So, instead of keeping score, or getting even, or looking good, the process is simply one of surrender."

"Of course. Simply surrender. And I'm surrendering to who?"

"Whom," he said.

"Okay, to *whom.*"

"To a power greater than yourself."

"To God?" I said.

"Or the Great Pumpkin."

"What about the Big Scorekeeper in the sky?"

"No such thing," he said.

"That's not what I heard."

"Of course that's not what you heard. The people who are making the rules are always trying to convince us that there's a Big Scorekeeper in the sky. They have an interest in doing just that. We can talk about that when we discuss the last and deadliest need: the Need to Control."

"You mean nobody's keeping score?"

"Not unless it's you," he said.

"Seems like there ought to be somebody up there . . ."

"Oh, there is. Somebody. Not judging or keeping score, though. Somebody paying attention. Minding the store. You remember that thing from the Bible about, *Not a sparrow falls from the sky but that your heavenly Father knows.* Remember that?"

"Vaguely."

"Well, somebody told me that the way God *knows* about the sparrow is because God *is* the sparrow."

"Do you realize that you said God again? And it's happened more than once in the last few weeks."

"You promise not to tell, I'll say it again."

"Scout's honor," I said.

"God. And don't tell anybody; it'll ruin my reputation as an agnostic."

"I'm almost speechless. This is like being present for some very important event."

"People mistake being irreverent for being an agnostic. The two are not necessarily related."

"Oh."

"But you get the idea?" he said. "About the sparrow?"

"I think so. You mean everything is holy in some way? Maybe that's not the right word. Too religious. Everything is . . ."

"Everything is connected. It's like there's no outside of things. Everything's inside."

"Inside of what?" I said.

"Put your hands over your ears," he said.

I actually started to do that before I realized what I was doing.

"Come on."

"Inside God."

"Jesus, Tyler."

"Scout's honor," he said. "Inside God."

"Man . . ."

"*In a dark time, the eye begins to see.* Remember who said that?"

"Don't tell me," I said. "American poet . . . eh . . ."

"Starts with an *R*."

"That's it. Roethke. Theodore Roethke. But what does it mean? Everything's inside."

"For one thing, it means that Somebody actually *is* minding the store and fortunately it's not me. Or you. It means that there's no real need to keep score anymore. Mistakes may not be possible; they may never have been possible. It means that my job consists of just showing up every day. Just being there."

"And just where is there?" I said.

"There is wherever you are. Bloom where you're planted. My job is to suit up and show up. I once heard a lady say that her job was to load the wagon, not worry about whether the mule went blind."

"Meaning?"

"Get out of the results business. If your job is to load the wagon, just load it and don't worry about the mule—that's not your department. The results will take care of themselves. And the score. Don't keep checking to see what the score is. It doesn't matter. Chop wood and carry water. Mother Teresa said that if you want the lamp to burn, you have to keep adding oil. The basics. Just add the oil. Suit up and show up. It's like the lottery—*must be present to win.* Don't keep taking your pulse. If you're loading the wagon, just load it. Leave the mule to the Mule Department. I'm told we have very capable people in the Mule Department."

"And the score's not important?"

"It's of no consequence," he said. "None."

"Don't tell the bookies," I said.

"The bookies already know," he said. "It's the gamblers you'll have to tell."

He lit a cigarette and looked up at the light over the table.

"You know what Winnie-the-Pooh said about keeping score?" he said.

"No idea."

"He said, *Although eating honey was a very good thing to do, there was a moment before you began to eat it which was better than when you were, but he didn't know what it was called."*

"Foreplay?"

"Jesus, Edward . . ."

"That supposed to be about keeping score?"

"It's about life," he said. "The journey. Same thing."

"I'm not sure I'm getting this."

"It'll sink in. Probably make more sense next week. Or next year. Also some degree of patience may be required."

"Not my strong suit," I said.

"Nor mine," he said.

"Next week's the need to control?"

"It is. The final week."

"Man. The time goes quick, eh?"

"Quickly," he said.

"Okay, quickly. Jesus."

"I'm a one-man committee trying to preserve adverbs in the English language. Things like *dress warm* and *drive slow* set my teeth on edge."

"I'll miss our time together," I said.

"Me, too," he said. "But on to next week."

"Loading the wagon?"

"Right," he said.

"And we don't care if the mule goes blind."

"Not our department. We let the Mule Department worry about that. They have to work, too."

He got up and shuffled toward the door. He looked very old.

"The need to control," he said, shaking his head. "Very deadly. *Ve-ry* deadly."

Seven

The Need to Control

Man cannot discover new oceans until he has the courage to lose sight of the shore.

—Anonymous

You know the stock market's going in the tank, Tyler? Right in the tank. Along with my investments. My security. My entire financial future."

"You making coffee?" he said. "I thought I smelled coffee."

"I'm making it, Tyler. I'm making it. Jesus . . . You're so impatient sometimes."

"I know. Bad character defect. You know what I say sometimes when I recite the Serenity Prayer?"

"No."

"I say, God grant me the serenity to accept my character defects."

"You think that's maybe a cop-out?" I said. "Perhaps an excuse for being so insensitive? Unwilling to try to improve?"

95

"Possibly," he said.

"I mean my future is spiraling down the toilet along with the rest of the stock market and you're worried about the goddam coffee."

"I say something wrong?"

"Yes, you said something wrong."

"What was it?" he said.

"Well, I said my financial future in the stock market was in extreme jeopardy. Extreme. Going in the tank big time. And all you could say was, *Where's the coffee?*"

"Oh . . . But you see we can *do* something about the coffee, Edward. One of the few things we can control—when we make the coffee. We can do that. We can't do anything about the stock market. But worry, maybe."

"So I'm not supposed to be worried?"

"Waste of time worrying about things you can't control."

"Jesus . . . That's a very insensitive thing to say, Tyler."

"Really?"

"Really," I said. "Shows a definite lack of compassion. Buddha would not be pleased."

"Sorry. Mind if I smoke?" he said.

"Actually, I do mind if you smoke, but that never stops you from smoking. Didn't stop Ann from smoking either. If I get lung cancer and die, I'm coming back to haunt both of you. Trust me, this is no idle threat."

"I left my smokes at home."

"Jesus . . ."

I got one of the two remaining packs out of the cupboard and gave it to him. He snapped the filter off one of the cigarettes and lit it. I don't know why but it irritates me no end that he snaps the filters off.

"I've got a question for you," he said.

"Shoot."

"Who said, *We don't see things as they are, we see things as we are?*"

"Peter Pan?"

"No."

"Peter Rabbit?"

"No."

"I give up, Tyler. I give up."

"Anaïs Nin."

"Imagine. I never would have guessed. Well, there goes my shot at Double Jeopardy."

"Did you have a nice week?" he said, frowning at the cigarette.

"Not world-class."

"I had a dream about you and Sweet Pamela," he said.

"Did you now."

"I did," he said.

"And?"

"And what?"

"You going to tell me about it or did you just want to tell me that you *had* the dream?"

"We're doing the need to control this week," he said.

"I know that. The dream . . . ?"

"It was about control issues," he said.

"The dream was?"

"Yeah."

"I should have known."

"Why? Could have been about anything."

"But it just happened to be about control issues," I said. "Funny how it worked out like that. And just on the week we were going to talk about that very thing."

"Life is sometimes full of strange coincidences."

"I've heard that," I said.

"The dream took place in a restaurant. You had just ordered oatmeal for breakfast."

"I never eat oatmeal."

"In the dream, Edward," he said. "In the dream."

"Okay."

"You ordered oatmeal, and they brought you runny, half-cooked eggs."

"You sure it was me in the restaurant?" I said.

"I never forget a customer."

"I hate runny eggs. I like them scrambled. Scrambled well."

"I know. You got angry and sent them back," he said.

"Good for me. Were you the waiter?"

"I don't think so," he said. "Seems like I was just watching all this."

"Then what happened?"

"The scene shifted."

"And the plot thickened?" I said.

"No plot, Edward. It was just a dream."

"Go on."

"You were driving a semi."

"I love trucks . . . *Oooogah!* . . . *Oooogah!*"

"I know. You were driving in the mountains, late for a delivery."

"Man, I hope I was hurrying. What was in the truck?"

"I'm not sure, but I think it was Halloween masks."

"Halloween masks? I had a semi full of Halloween masks?"

"Yeah," he said. "Either that or plumbing fixtures."

"Tyler . . ."

"You were going down this hill way too fast and the brakes gave out."

"I was in serious trouble. No brakes and I'm going downhill."

"Faster and faster, barely making it around the curves. You were leaning on the horn."

"*Oooogah! Oooogah!*"

"That's it. But it was no use. In a fit of panic, you resorted to prayer."

"I did?"

"Yes. You said, *God help me.* I think it was actually *God please help me.* You yelled it at the top of your lungs. Your heart was pumping like crazy. Your eyes were wide open, taking everything in. You were in full-panic mode."

"Good for me," I said. "That was probably the right response."

"Then a voice said . . . *Let* . . ."

"A voice?"

"A voice," he said.

"Where'd the voice come from?"

"How would I know where the voice came from?"

"But you're trying to tell me it was the voice of God," I said.

"I'm not trying to tell you anything," he said. "I'm talking about the dream."

"You're just sharing with me. About the dream."

"Right. Sharing. So the voice said, *Let go of the steering wheel.*"

"This was the voice of some lunatic, right?"

"I don't know," he said. "But he said it three times."

"And did I let go of the wheel?"

"No," he said.

"So what happened?"

"You didn't make it around one of those curves. Truck turned over and burst into flames. You never had a chance."

"All those Halloween masks."

"Or plumbing fixtures."

"Man . . . what a terrible dream."

"Yeah," he said. "Really sad."

"So you think I should've let go of the steering wheel?"

"Beats me," said Tyler.

"Wouldn't make sense to let go of the wheel, though, would it?"

"Not hardly. But then it wasn't going real well."

"Really well," I said.

"Really well?"

"Yeah."

"Huh . . . But then it wasn't going really well when you *did* have hold of the wheel."

"No, but I mean that's going from a slim chance to no chance."

"You ever hear about the guy who was hanging on to this little shrub of a plant on the side of a cliff above a thousand-foot drop."

"No, but I know you're going to tell me about him."

"Guy was in dire straits, like you in the dream, and he asked for help. Prayed actually. *If there's anybody up there, please help me.*"

"I am overwhelmed by the similarities between these two stories," I said.

"And he, too, heard a voice that said *Let go.*"

"Did he let go?"

"He thought about it for a few minutes and then said, *Is there anybody else up there?*"

"Oh, Tyler, that's so bad. I can't believe you actually . . ."

"So what's the nature of the lesson, Edward?"

"Check the brakes on your truck before you head for the mountains?"

"The nature of the lesson, Star Pupil, is that the need to control can be deadly."

"So does that mean I'm supposed to listen to every . . ."

"It means that when your way doesn't work, when to continue on the same path will surely lead to destruction, it may be wise to try it someone else's way."

"I don't think it would be wise to listen to all the voices in my head, Tyler. You have no idea how many there are."

"Oh, but I do know," he said. "That's the beauty of living in community with people who have similar problems with strange voices and aberrant behavior."

"You know, that's what Son of Sam did," I said. "Remember Son of Sam? He listened to all those voices in his head and ended up killing a bunch of people because they told him to. The voices did. Sometimes voices in *my* head tell me to do that. *That guy on the freeway that just cut you off would be better off dead.*"

"And the major difference is that you don't act on it. You actually recognize it, not as the voice of God, but as the voice of some enormously self-destructive part of yourself."

"So when I'm coming down the mountain in my truck without brakes and this voice says, *Let go of the steering wheel,* I should do that?"

"Yes," he said. "And the reason you would do that is because?"

"Because I have an I.Q. of about sixty?"

"Wrong. The reason you would do that is because *your way's not working.* Having decided that the brakes weren't going to start working any time soon, it might have occurred to you that you were no longer in control, and some other action might be appropriate."

"But . . . let go of the wheel?"

"Why not? You've got nothing to lose. Perhaps extreme measures are required. You think *surrender to win* makes any more sense?

"So I'm not really in control?"

"Never were," he said. "Control's an illusion. The need to control is fear-based. What's the opposite of fear?"

"Faith?"

"What's the opposite of control?"

"Surrender?"

"Go to the head of the class, Edward," said Tyler.

"My job's just to suit up and show up?"

"Perfect. And believe. Stay out of the control business. It's deadly."

"And by the way, for the record, I don't see myself as someone who has trouble with aberrant behavior."

"As part of your continuing education, Edward, I would suggest that drinking shaving lotion, and breaking open nasal inhalers to ingest the contents comes as close to aberrant behavior as you want to get."

"But . . ."

"It's not important, Edward. It's just information. I was once caught wearing ladies' undies during something of a minor crime spree. Trying to earn a little pocket money for another bottle of wine that I desperately needed at the moment. Very embarrassing."

"You were? You never told me that."

"More will be revealed," he said. "Let's just go on."

"So, I'm going to act on this completely irrational suggestion and just let go? That the deal?"

"That's it," he said. "Just let go."

"Tyler, that's what crazy people do."

"You ever hear about Crazy Wisdom?"

"No," I said.

"It's wisdom that doesn't make any sense. Wisdom without linearity or logic. Divine wisdom. You remember the thing about, *Let go and let God?*"

"I do."

"That's it."

"What's it?"

"If you've been doing your part, the suit up and show up part, the part where you clean up your side of the street and stop worrying about everybody else's side, then you'll be given the wisdom you need. *That* wisdom. Every day you get a fresh supply. Sometimes several times a day. It will not be necessarily linear or logical. It's the wisdom of children and small animals. Receive it in the spirit of play. And, Mister Bear, as a special bonus, you'll be given the grace to stay out of the control business. Someone with much greater vision is directing the show."

"Would that happen to be God?" I said.

Tyler gave me his who-could-possibly-know shrug.

"A possibility," was all he would say.

"So what was the first part of the dream about? All the stuff in the restaurant about oatmeal and runny eggs. What was that all about?"

"Dreams are funny like that. Sometimes they don't make a bit of sense."

"You know, I worry about you, Tyler. I really do. There are times when I think you've actually gone round the bend, are even now in La-La Land, dining with the Out-to-Lunch Bunch."

"Well, I think it's nice that you worry about me," he said. "It's comforting in some strange way. But there's no need to, really. You see, I'm protected by a Benevolent Force in the Universe, and nothing can harm me."

"Nothing can harm you? That what you said?"

"I did."

"You've gone back to being bulletproof? Like in the old days?"

"Perhaps I should have said that nothing can injure me," he said. "And I'm certainly not bulletproof. As a matter of fact, plenty of bullets still get in, but . . ."

"So the bullet holes are for what? Ventilation?"

"Reminders that I'm human."

"Ahhhh . . . human."

"You remember human," he said. "It's what we're trying to become more of."

"I thought we were trying to become more spiritual."

"We are. But you get more spiritual by becoming more human."

"Oh . . . Of course you realize that that makes no sense."

"I do."

"You think possibly that years of taking drugs and drinking to excess has perhaps fried a few too many brain cells?"

"I could believe that."

"Tyler, Tyler . . . Okay. So say that I have now managed somehow to acquire all this faith and have surrendered and am completely out of the control business, how will I know what to do?"

"Simple. You ask for directions," he said.

"Ask who?"

"The Great Pumpkin, Jesus, God, Allah . . . Doesn't make any difference."

"It doesn't?"

"No."

"Why?"

"Because it's all the same stuff," he said. "Divine stuff."

"Man, oh man . . ."

Tyler glanced at his watch.

"Time to go," he said.

"You're going to leave me in the middle of *everything's divine stuff?*"

"The best possible place."

"How am I going to find out what that means?" I said.

"You ask. Didn't we just go over all that?"

"We skimmed over it at best. An outline maybe. A bare outline."

"But of course, Edward, that's all you need. This Presence in the Universe will supply the rest. The Force."

"Ah, the Force. I remember the Force. *Star Wars.*"

"That's it."

"So let me get this straight. My job is just to ask? Suit up, show up and ask? That's all there is to it?"

"Oh, just because it's simple doesn't mean it's easy, Noble Student. It's actually fairly difficult to suit up and show up on a regular basis. You know, like every day. Breathing in and out and looking for the spaces between thoughts for thirty minutes a day is not all that easy."

"I'm supposed to be looking for the spaces *between* thoughts?"

"Right. The empty spaces."

"Jesus God . . . the empty spaces."

He got up from the table.

"You heading for the laundry?" I said.

"My next stop."

"Be careful. Lots of crazies over there."

"That's why I go; it's where I belong. Besides, nothing can harm me. You know that," he paused. "I love you, Edward. Remember that. It's the great gift we have for one another."

"I've almost got all the sessions typed up. What will I do when I get done?"

"Ask for directions," he said.

"You're impossible," I said.

"I certainly hope so. And don't forget about gratitude and forgiveness."

"I know, I know. The two most important spiritual practices."

"Good night," he said. "Sleep well."

"Good night. I'll call tomorrow. You be home?"

"Probably. If I'm not, somebody will answer. May take a while. Just keep trying. That's the key."

"And suit up and show up."

"Right," he said. "You know what Thomas Mann said about love?"

"No idea."

"It's from *Magic Mountain*. He said, *It's love, not reason, that's stronger than death.*"

"More heart and less thinking?"

"That's the lesson," said Tyler.

"I'm very confused."

"Good. Confusion is the first step toward wisdom."

"Who would've guessed? Good night, Tyler. I love you."

"Thank you. The feeling is shared and returned tenfold. That's the way love works."

CPSIA information can be obtained
at www.ICGtesting.com
Printed in the USA
LVHW081954271220
675131LV00059B/3306